Praise for Hans Holst Andersen's
Along the Margins

Hans Holst Andersen completed his novel "for its own sake," and a colleague stated, "It would be unfortunate if such essentially American culture material should not reach a general audience."

His granddaughter and editor says, "This is an absolute gem of a novel. Read it. You will love it!"

— Liz J. Andersen

Along
The Margins

SOUTH DAKOTA IMMIGRANT HOMESTEADERS

Along The Margins

SOUTH DAKOTA IMMIGRANT HOMESTEADERS

A Novel by

Hans Holst Andersen

Labbwerk Publishing
Eugene

Labbwerk Publishing, Eugene 97404

Labbwerk Publishing gratefully acknowledges the generous of support of:
Anders Andersen: cover landscape and back cover portrait oil paintings
Liz J. Andersen, Brian J. Boudler, & Jackie Melvin: editors
All Photographs from the personal collection of Hans and Pauline Andersen

Andersen, Hans Holst

Along the Margins: South Dakota Immigrant Homesteaders
A Novel by Hans Holst Andersen
Eugene, Oregon :
Labbwerk Publishing, 2022
p. : illustrations ; cm.
Summary: Erik left a bleak life and livelihood in Denmark, and abandoned his aspiration to become an artist, to immigrate to America. Working as a farmhand on a rural homestead in South Dakota, he found hard work, suffering, heartbreak, and terrible loneliness. He also found an awe-inspiring landscape, and good people who wouldn't let him give up on his art. Would he stake his own claim there or pursue his art? He came to America to "find himself." Would he succeed? Hans H. Andersen wrote this semi-autobiographical novel and like Erik, immigrated through Ellis Island at age 18, speaking only Danish, and earned his way on South Dakota homesteads. Yet he earned a degree in English and French from Iowa State Teachers College and a Doctorate in Philosophy at the University of Chicago. Andersen taught English Literature and Composition, heading the Department of English, Foreign Languages, and Speech at Oklahoma at A&M.

Library of Congress Control Number: 2022936329

ISBN 978-0-9988448-2-4 (paperback)
ISBN 978-0-9988448-3-1 (ebook)

1. United States -- Emigration and immigration -- 20th century -- Fiction. 2. Immigrants -- Cultural assimilation -- Fiction. 4. Farmers – South Dakota – Fiction. 6. Farm life – Fiction. 7. Man-woman relationships – Fiction. 8. South Dakota – Fiction.

FOR THE
ANDERSEN FAMILY

This story begins in 1913.

1

A farm wagon clattered slowly down the curve that evening.

"That's our son Chris coming now," Mayland said.

Erik's eyes followed the wagon. A white horse hauled on the near side.

"Got a load of posts," Mayland said. "Going to do some fencing. To make the pasture bigger."

"The pasture." Erik nodded, his mouth dry. "I see." The change would begin soon.

The wagon stopped by Mayland's corral, and Chris climbed down and tied up the team, before coming toward his father and Erik. Chris was stocky, shorter than Erik, slightly stooped in his wash-faded blue overalls and matching jacket, and wore a hat.

"Hi," Mayland called. "Got somebody for you."

"Yeah? That's good." Chris held Erik's hand in a large, hard grip. "Had a nice trip?"

"Ye-es," Erik said, noticing the whites of Chris's eyes in his sun-darkened face.

"Won't you come in?" Mayland said to Chris.

"Naw, guess not tonight. Have to be gettin' back. Still got the chores to do."

"Well." Mayland looked from one to the other. "The boy here is ready, I guess. Got his overalls and things." He turned to Erik. "Better get 'em then," Mayland said, opening the porch screen door for Erik.

"Mother all right?" Erik heard Chris ask.

Erik thought he should say goodbye to her, but the silent expectancy of the two men seemed to give him no chance. Probably he would see both Mayland and Martha again soon, anyway. Erik picked up his bundle and suitcase from the porch swing, where he'd left them after riding with Mayland from the train station and town.

"Come back over when you can," Mayland said, still holding the screen door open.

Chris took Erik's suitcase. "Well, we'll be going then, I guess."

Mayland nodded. "Be seeing you."

"So long," Chris said.

"So long." Mayland let the screen door bang shut.

The only sound after that was Chris and Erik's footsteps crunching on gravel. Erik had to hurry to keep up with Chris. This was when the change would begin to touch Erik personally. He carried clothes like Chris's in the bundle under his arm. Tomorrow he would put them on and start to look like Chris. He noticed spools of barbed wire on top of fence poles in the wagon, and remembered the endless fences he'd seen from his train window along the track and in the fields. It probably took a long time to set a post on a raw windy day, digging a hole in the hard ground, and tamping the dirt back in.

Chris stepped up on a wheel hub to find a place for Erik's suitcase and then reached down for his bundle. "You can git up," he said, and then climbed down and walked around to untie the horses.

They drove up the curve, turning east toward the town, which was built on a shelf fronting the river bottom, its back against the slope of a divide to the north. The white mare, Sally, kept lagging behind, and Chris slapped her with the line, but only spirited on her teammate instead, a willing bay called Prince.

"So you just came this afternoon," Chris said. "Father expected you sooner, I guess."

Erik nodded. "My ship was late."

"That so?"

"On account of a storm," Erik added.

"Oh."

Erik waited. Apparently Chris didn't want to know more about it. He sat looking straight ahead. He had a strong face, the face of a man who knew what he wanted, and Erik couldn't help feeling some envy. He'd just completed a journey half way around the world in search of a new purpose.

Erik found himself studying Chris's features, as if for answers. There seemed to be no hint of Mayland or Martha in Chris. He wasn't like his brother either. Al was the easy-going kind, from what Erik had seen of him that afternoon. The kind who liked to dramatize himself too. Erik realized he was staring, and in his mind going through the preliminaries to making a sketch. He quickly looked away.

Chris seemed to read his mind. "The folks tell me you used to paint in the old country."

"Ye-es. A little." Erik didn't want to talk about it. He didn't even want to think about it.

But Chris had chosen his Danish words with difficulty, and they both struggled to find something to say. Erik realized this was the way it would be until he learned English, with only Chris to talk to. His wife didn't know Danish and neither did their daughter. What were their names?

"But you was raised on a farm?" Chris asked next. "That's what Father said."

Erik nodded.

"O' course, it's gonna be a little different here, I expect." Chris looked at him.

"Yes, I know."

Off to the left, against the slope by the railroad track, a grain elevator with galvanized sides rose stiffly. Then they passed coal sheds and the depot, like the other towns Erik had ridden through. It was about this time last night his train had finally crossed the Missouri River into Nebraska. As his train veered northwest toward South Dakota, he'd sat watching the flat country gliding into darkness, the soiled streaks of snowdrifts in the right-of-way, the flickering telegraph poles, and now and then a lonely light from a farmhouse.

This was a new town, laid out on Mayland's land, and named after him. It had come with an irrigation project and the railroad. Mayland had invested too much in it and was again living on his old ranch nearby, tending his cow, chickens, and apple orchard. But he actually had a town named after him. He'd had a hand in all of this. Back home, people knew about it, and even speculated that he had maybe also built the railroad. He had left Denmark as a poor immigrant, but in America everything was possible.

This was why Erik had also come. To begin again, where anything was possible. He could forget about his desire to become an artist, forget about being something for which he had some talent, maybe. Yet no more than many people who would never think of trying to make a living by it. People who made art for fun, just because they wanted to. But Erik knew there was a difference between wanting to paint a picture and feeling driven to paint it.

That sounded like something his artist friend Brandt would have told him, but it wasn't. Brandt had said something else when Erik first told him about going to America. Something that hurt. To Brandt's "What for?" Erik had said, "To find myself."

Brandt had looked at him with his wise blue eyes, shook his head, and made Erik face a painful truth. "My friend, once again you're only giving the same answer as everyone else, just like you do in your paintings. But becoming more involved in yourself won't make you or your work any more original. I think what you need is quite the opposite–to find something outside yourself. To look out and not in. To lose yourself, I might say, in something bigger than yourself.

"It's possible America can help with that. I think maybe it can. There you'll be on the receiving end of things for a while. You won't even be able to talk back."

Of course Erik didn't have to stay in South Dakota. He just happened to start here because his folks knew the Maylands. It was a place to go, and, as it turned out, he could work for Chris, at least this summer. And here he was now, on the last lap, riding on a lumber wagon in Dakota. He watched their reflection slide across the slate-colored store windows of Main Street, a block and a half of narrow frame buildings, false fronts facing each other over plank walkways.

The road turned north and crossed the train tracks, and Erik looked toward the low, flat-roofed train station, now deserted and dead. A dim light glowed by the switch. Some day, he thought, he would return here, to travel back through the valley, and south along the Black Hills. He glanced over his shoulder back at them, standing darkly against the whole southwestern horizon, and coming to a peak in the center.

Sally's shoes sparked on the grade, and a basin flecked with alkali slowly appeared over the top of the slope. Beyond it lay a cluster of knolls, with a farmhouse on the west side. Could this be it? Chris sat immobile, looking off to the other side at the flat alkali stretches reaching on and on to the edge of darkness. The wagon rolled on across the basin and up through the knolls. And then Erik saw another divide out ahead, naked and wrinkled, with the wooded course of a creek directly below.

Chris pointed. "You can see it now."

A small farmstead stood by itself, on the foot of the divide, above the treetops. The team set into a trot downhill. Erik held onto the edge of the seat, his fingers growing cold. He should have heeded Mayland's advice about buying some gloves. Erik had arrived in March, but spring must come later here. The jarring in the ruts went straight to his temples, and he raised chilled hands to press them.

Chris glanced at him. "Father say anything about wages?"

Erik nodded, while grabbing back onto the edge of the seat. "He wrote about it."

"Yeah, we talked it over, and thought maybe twenty-five dollars a month would be about right."

"Yes," Erik quickly agreed. It seemed unbelievable he could earn so much.

"'Course, you'll be kinda new at things for a while."

"Yes."

Chris promptly changed the subject. "This is our land all along here." He waved his hand.

Light drained out of the sky and dusk filled the hollows. Only the divide seemed to hold out against the night. The wagon crossed a bridge and crawled up an unfenced road, turning off on a trail to the left across some gullies. Chris kept his foot on the brake lever.

They came to a barbed-wire fence on a rise, and Erik jumped down to open the gate. It looked like a piece of the fence, the wires strung from one of the gate posts to a stick, which in turn was held to the other post with wire loops. The wires were tight, and Erik pulled, jerked, and pried. But the top loop had to come off first, and it clung stubbornly to its groove, and his fingers felt numb. He looked helplessly up at Chris, who promptly wrapped his lines around the brake handle and came down over the doubletree.

"A little tight, huh?" Chris gripped the stick, and drew it loose instantly. "Better git back on the wagon."

Erik climbed back up, intensely miserable. He wasn't worth twenty-five dollars. He would be new at things. He had always been new at things. He drove through, and the wires twanged behind him. Then Chris climbed back on and took the reins again.

The trail sank into a ravine. When they came out on the other side Erik could see Chris's house, a shack with a lean-to on the north. A flue rose from it like a mast, with baling-wire rigging. A fence surrounded the house, too heavy and close, like a fence around a haystack to keep animals out.

Chris drove straight to the barn, and they unhitched in silence, which was a chore near the end of Erik's long day. They unhooked the doubletree traces from the horses' collars and harnesses, which they also took off the horses. Erik followed Chris into the barn, each loaded with a collar and harness, and put it all away. Then they led the horses to the creek for water. Chris had cut the bank down for a crossing to his fields. It also made a shortcut to the crossroads at the knolls, Chris explained, impassable only when snow drifted in, or in heavy downpours, or when spill-water from the irrigation reservoir swelled the creek.

The stable inside the barn was dark, but the horses and Chris knew their way. Chris said the rest of the chores could wait until after supper. On the way to the house they walked past an old woodshed, and Erik was briefly surprised to learn he would sleep there. He hadn't thought about where he'd stay, but the house certainly looked too small. Erik glanced back at the wagon, where he'd left his suitcase and bundle.

"You can git 'em later," Chris said. "Julie's got supper ready I expect."

Their house was warm inside and smelled of fried potatoes and onions.

"Anybody home?" Chris called in English.

A noise came from the front room, and a small woman entered the kitchen.

"Oh, hello. I'm Julia." She held out her hand and Erik took it briefly. "Erik, isn't it?" she said in a soft voice. He nodded and she took his cap. "Bren-ding?" she ventured.

"Ye-es."

"Oh." Chris took off his jacket and hat. "That your last name?"

"Sure," Julia said.

Chris turned to the washstand, dipped water into the basin, and drank from the dipper. "Go ahead and wash up," he said in Danish.

Erik pushed his sleeves back and crowded sideways, to get out of Chris's shadow. When Erik finished, Chris emptied the basin through the door and refilled it for himself. Julia busied herself with the table, but paused to motion Erik to a chair at the other end. Erik hung his coat on the back of his chair and sat down. The screen door suddenly slammed and their daughter rushed in, stopping abruptly.

"Louise," her mother said, "come and meet Erik." Chris translated.

Louise stepped forward with the cool outdoors on her. "Hello," she said, holding out her hand to him, and he took it and nodded wordlessly.

She would sit next to him, Erik saw, as Chris sat down at the other end. Erik felt too warm sitting near the stove. On a shelf, between small windows looking out on the divide, a clock ticked, and the bright disk of the pendulum swung behind decorated glass. Julia was watching Erik, and he glanced toward Chris. A lamp stood right between them. "You milk many cows?" Erik asked too loudly, and Julia and Louise turned their heads simultaneously. For a moment he was still afraid Chris hadn't heard.

"Naw," Chris drawled. "Seven right now."

Julia said something.

"She wants to know if you can milk," Chris again translated.

"A little," Erik said, and Chris translated for his wife.

Julia nodded approvingly, and then talk stalled again. "Tea?" she finally asked each in turn.

"Naw." Chris was the first to get up. "Expect you're tired," Chris said to Erik.

Chris put his jacket and hat back on and lit a lantern. Erik stood up, put his coat back on, Julia handed him his cap, and he followed Chris out. They crossed in the circle of the lantern light to the woodshed. It stood apart as if it didn't quite belong. Resting on a slope, the shed was propped up on cement blocks at the south end, and wooden steps led up to the door.

"Kind of stuffy in here, I expect," Chris said. "It ain't been used lately."

The musty air met them at the door and carried a strong smell of harness. The bed stood to the left, a double iron bed with tall gate-like ends. The shed had no real ceiling right above the ribs of two-by-four joists. Harnesses, old shirts, and overalls draped the walls. A wooden arm held out a string of horse collars, and a saddle lay on its side on the floor beside the bed.

Chris jerked open a window in the east wall, revealing it from under a sagging piece of yellow curtain. He moved a pair of rubber boots from the top of a cardboard box to let the window fully swing in.

"Kind of messy. A feller oughta git it cleaned up sometime." Chris took another lantern from a nail, shook it, and set it on an up-ended orange crate. "Oh, yeah," he said as he lit it, "you still ain't got your stuff yet."

Chris had to go back inside the house while Erik retrieved his suitcase and bundle, and then he waited by the steps. It grew colder, with a breeze blowing off the divide. He found the Big Dipper and drew a line to the North Star. Still the familiar stars over this new and lonely land. The kitchen door opened and Chris came back out with milk pails. Erik moved to join him.

"Naw, better not tonight, in your good suit. It won't take long." Chris started to go. "Got your things?"

"Yes."

"Well, better go to bed then. Didn't get much sleep on the train, I expect."

Erik slowly turned back. Chris was right. Erik hadn't been out of his best suit or slept solidly for days–ever since the early morning he had hurried up on deck to see America for the first time–dim globes along the shore and shuttling ferryboats. He had to hang his Sunday suit and cap on a nail tonight. The bed felt hard, and after a little while he pushed the stifling, dusty covers away from his face. The air from the open window barely reached him.

When he closed his eyes he felt as if he was on the train as if it stood still, waiting for another to pass. He dreamily remembered school lessons about southern states, where Lincoln had fought to free the slaves. Light flared through the window as Chris passed on his way to the house, and the shadows of the skeleton joists chased each other across the rafters above, holding up the thin roof. The screen door banged closed, and Erik felt again as if he was riding the rocking and speeding train.

Chris's hard knuckles rapped on the door and woke Erik up. He slid from under his quilts and closed the window. A draft kept billowing the yellow curtain, letting in faint light, sliding up and down the wall. Erik heard the barn door slam, and a muffled crowing. His new overalls were too long in the legs, even though he was tall, and he had to turn them up. Mayland had said they would shrink in the wash. Apparently overalls were expected to fit only in a general way. The jacket felt thin and his fingers numb on the brass buttons, pressing them through hard slits. He hurried down to the barn.

He pulled the door against the wind just enough to squeeze in, and walked through the stale-warm stable, to the corral where Chris was milking.

"I guess you can groom the horses and clean out their stalls first," Chris said. "Then water the horses."

Erik turned back, conscious of Chris's eyes following his stiff overalls, the big cuffs rubbing each other.

He got cold on his trips to the creek with the horses. The sky was ash-colored, and smoke fled horizontally from the flue. Maybe the weather would be too bad for fencing. When Erik returned to the stable, Chris stuck his head in. "You want to try milking one?"

Thankfully Bess was an easy milker, and she felt warm against him. Erik couldn't make the milk foam in the pail as he knew he should, but when he poured it into the can, Chris gave an approving nod. "Yeah, that's about what she gives of a morning now." He removed the strainer and clanked on the lid, and they carried the can between them around the corral to the separator room.

"Feels almost like it might snow." Chris peered into the leaden sky.

Erik nodded hopefully.

But nothing came of it. After breakfast they loaded tools, harnessed the team, brought them out, and hooked their traces to the doubletree still attached to the wagon. Chris stopped abruptly. "Git that neckyuck," he ordered, with a nod of his head.

"Neckyuck?" Erik said. Chris didn't know the Danish word for it?

"Over there!" Chris pointed in the direction of a disk plow standing alongside the corral.

Erik hurried toward it and looked for anything loose, then hesitatingly back at Chris. Chris suddenly picked up a wooden rod, with a metal ring in the middle and a smaller metal ring at each end, from his wagon, and flung it toward the corral. The team reared, only to be jerked back instantly with a loud cumulative curse from Chris.

Erik, now completely flustered and feeling compelled to make some kind of move, picked up the roughly meter long wood rod with rings that Chris had thrown.

"Hell no!" Chris strode over and jerked the center ring of a second neckyoke from the tapered end of the long wooden tongue of the disk. "This one here." He visibly tried to steady his voice. "That other ain't no good. Damn thing came off in the lumberyard. Gotta git it fixed."

Chris inserted the end of the long wagon tongue into the center ring of the neckyoke, and attached its end rings to the front of Sally and Prince's collars. Chris and Erik climbed up on the wagon. Chris drove it on the trail over which they had come the night before. Erik raised the short collar of his jacket, crouched against the wind, covered his ears with his hands, and wished again he had some gloves. Not holding on, he kept sliding against Chris, who broke his silence only with spasmodic gestures to keep Sally from lagging behind. The wrinkled slope lay bleak against the clouds.

Chris opened the gate again. Here they left the trail and followed the fence up the divide. A jack rabbit tore out of hiding and fled sideways into a ravine. "Purdy rough country," Chris said. "Makes a little feed if you got enough of it." He explained he wanted to run the pasture another half-mile north. He would set the posts himself while Erik took down the old fence at the end. When they reached the east corner, Chris helped him get started.

Chris watched Erik fumble with the pliers. "Don't you have any gloves?"

Erik shook his head.

"You'll sure need 'em. Better take mine."

"But you'll need them yourself," Erik protested, as Chris pulled them off.

"Naw. You can't roll wire with bare hands, that's a cinch." He handed his gloves to Erik. "Kind of big for you, I expect."

They were leather gloves, with no lining, but still felt warm from Chris's hands. The staples stuck hard in the dry posts, and Erik pulled and twisted and broke them. The wind constantly threatened to take his cap, and his roomy overalls alternately inflated and flapped around his legs. His fingers grew numb in their pod-like casings, and he beat his hands hard against his body and then raised them to cover his chilled ears. He gazed down the slope to the creek and across the bottoms to the knolls. Low clouds blotted out the Black Hills.

It was a long time until noon, and then an equally long afternoon, the stubby train coming down across the flats and leaving again. Then back to chores again, and another night in the woodshed, only to wake to more days like this.

Erik finally reached the west end of the pasture, and he turned around to roll up the loose wire. At first the loops kept falling apart. The wind now blew in his face, sweeping in unobstructed over the breaks. Then it began snowing. The particles drove hard and stinging, but gradually grew flaky and wet. Only the gullies gave a little shelter, and these became increasingly difficult to cross with the thickening hoop. Rising from the ground, the barbed wire ripped at dead tufts and braided them in a wreath.

From the ridges Erik could see Chris extending his line of posts northward. Chris never stopped to warm his hands or rest. Instead he moved steadily, piercing holes in the ground with a long crowbar, sharpened posts, and drove them in with measured thuds. Intermittently came a loud "Whoa."

The progress of the team and this steady worker against the thin-strewn bluffs constantly reminded Erik of his own shortcomings. Here was the symbol of the pioneer, pushing farther and farther out to take possession of the land, and with bare hands. The earth belonged to men like Chris and his father. Erik could only follow in their tracks and borrow their gloves.

2

In the glare of the March sun, the divide looked like a piece of the moon. South Dakota. Dakota. Erik repeated the name aloud, lonely vowels between hard consonants. How often he had said it back home, and in his daydreams he'd built dugouts or log cabins, broke the prairie, planted corn, and driven his covered wagon to distant settlements. He had never guessed how loneliness would forebodingly creep over him, at night, when he went to bed and the house had gone dark and still.

It pursued him into the harsh daylight of his first Sunday alone here, and he turned to study the woodshed and the barn with its upright weathered boards, gray as the corral and the cottonwoods. Beyond the creek bottoms the gray land rose heavily, and above it lay the distant cold-blue range of the Black Hills with a peak in the center. This was Dakota.

Erik felt suddenly chilled and he returned to the warm kitchen. Now that he'd finished the morning chores, perhaps he should go over to Mayland's, as Chris had suggested. He could sit there, drink coffee in the quiet afternoon, and talk of home. Even after these many years Mayland and Martha still spoke about the old country. It took feelings a long time to make a new home. Or rather it took a new home a long time to make new feelings.

As for Chris, Julia, and Louise, Erik had seen their lives only from outside, except for the kitchen. They hadn't even invited him into the front room, "the parlor," they called it. The door from the kitchen to it stood ajar, and he stepped inside the parlor for the first time. It had the unused look of a roped-off room in a museum—a library table in the middle, straight chairs about the walls, a fireplace behind isinglass, and opposite it, between the bedroom doors a china cabinet with family photographs on top. Erik saw pictures of Mayland and Martha; Al, their other son, whom Erik had met that first afternoon; and Louise, at several different ages.

In the largest she straddled a pony like a boy, the hem of her skirt caught on the saddle horn. He guessed she was five or six then, and something had made her laugh, so she looked perfectly natural and adorable. Another showed her as a baby in Julia's arms. Julia had been pretty, too, small and dark, a distinct kind of beauty, like the miniature silhouettes on the wall.

Erik suddenly saw with his blue eyes, in the big mirror by the kitchen door, how red his face had become. The sun had also bleached his red hair, a source of tiresome jokes back home. Erik the Red. Would his face turn as brown here as Chris's? Erik wondered if the farm work would give his lean build the same hard muscles Chris had.

On the other side of the door, in the middle of the wall, was a tinted enlargement of Chris and Julia, clearly their wedding picture. Chris had looked handsome then, like he still did, when shaved and dressed for church. On each side of the photograph hung a small watercolor–one of a mountain waterfall forever stilled on its rocks, and the other a bald peak with pines at its base. Christmas card trees. He looked for the name in the corner, Julia M., very distinct. He gingerly stepped out of her secrets and the house.

The end of the barn lay in shadow when Erik crossed to the woodshed. He sat down on his bed and gazed vacantly at the discarded pieces of men and horses. How infinitely quiet it was out here, with only the thin voice of the breeze on his screen door. He moistened the chapped backs of his hands with his mouth, and at length dropped back on the bed and looked up at the rafters. He heard the train whistle. Soon the engine would work its way down across the flats, pulling two yellow coaches and a baggage car, and then it would go back again.

He realized he had fallen asleep when he came to and sat up with a start. Someone stood at his door.

"I thought maybe you'd be here," the stranger said, in Erik's own dialect. The man ducked inside and stuck out his hand. "Jes," he introduced himself. "Jes Ellisen. Maybe Al told you about me."

"No-o." Erik stood up and shook hands with him. "I'm Erik Brending."

"I seen Al uptown last week, and he said you was coming here, so I thought I'd drop by and say 'Hello.'" Jes sank down on the bed and set his hat down beside him. He wore a shabby suit with milk stains on his knees. His black hair stuck out over his ears. "Family out?"

Erik nodded and sat down beside him.

"Ya, gone to church and then visitin', I expect. I guess they don't stay home much Sundays if they can help it. Julia's got to be on the go all the time." Jes paused, crossing one thin leg over the other. "Well, how you like it here?"

"Oh, I haven't been here long," Erik said evasively.

Talk shifted to their homes and back again. Jes had lived in America seven years and worked a homestead west of town. "Just got in on it in time. Damn lucky." Jes had thin, cracked lips, over which he kept moving the tip of his tongue. "You're just a little late, I'm afraid."

Erik smiled feebly.

"I know," Jes said. "You think you won't stay. That's what I thought too when I first came over. But what's the use? No chance for a feller back home. Here I got a hundred and sixty right now."

Erik nodded silently. A hundred and sixty what?

"You bet," Jes said.

"Uh-huh."

"Ya." Jes nodded. "You bet. It's all right. Everything is going to be all right. But there ain't nothing in farming. You got to have milk cows. I got twenty right now. O' course, I don't have much in the way of buildings yet, but I'll be getting around to putting up a shack one of these days. Got to prove up on my claim this year."

"Doesn't it get lonesome?" Erik couldn't help asking.

"You darn right it gets lonesome. This ain't no way for a man to live. But what you gonna do? Not many girls around here. Darn few. And they wouldn't have you. Look at Al. Got a nice house in town and all, and there he sits by himself."

Erik couldn't think of anything more to say. Even when there were girls around back home, he'd been too shy to catch their attention. What chance did he have here?

"Oh, there's some nice girls." Jes noticed the look on Erik's face. "Take Louise here. She's a nice girl all right. But she's stuck up too, like the Mrs. I seen Louise up at Bates Hall last winter, acting like she didn't know a feller. Oh, she'd dance with Al and Fred, o' course, and fellers like that. I s'pose she'll go to the Hills as soon as she gets through high school. To the college up there, I mean."

He paused, and Erik suddenly realized Jes was waiting for an answer. "I don't know. I haven't heard."

"Naw," Jes dropped it. "I was just wondering. I guessed somebody musta said somethin' about it." He reached for his hat. It was black and turned up on the sides like a coal shovel. "Have to be gettin' along. I want to stop for the mail on my way back." He stood up and walked toward the door. "Maybe I'll get a housekeeper. Been thinking about it."

"Can you get one?"

"Sure. Oh, it ain't so darn easy. O' course, I got to build more first." He pushed the screen door open, and Erik followed him out. "Come up sometime. I'll tell Al to come by for you next time I see him. He ain't so darn busy." Jes picked up his horse's reins and swung into his saddle.

Erik watched him ride out of sight, his slim figure bobbing along the fence toward the knolls. After seven years, this was what it came to. A cow mooed mournfully from the creek bottoms. Erik stared back at Chris's house and the divide for a moment. Then he remembered his socks, hanging on a line between the lean-to and the outhouse, which stood off to the north like a sentinel box.

Chris drove on ahead. He had to go around to the bridge because of the seeder tied behind his wagon. Erik could take the disk through the creek. To hitch up three horses, Erik carefully hooked traces from their collars and harnesses to a doubletree and a single tree, hooked those to a triple tree, which he hooked up to the low, disk stub tongue. As he hitched up, he discovered the neckyoke was missing, and remembered Chris was using it for the wagon. Erik searched around and found another outside the toolshed. If it was the one Chris had thrown that first morning, he had no doubt Chris had repaired it. He had worked in the tool room on Saturday to get his equipment ready. Erik saw nothing wrong with the neckyoke and finished hitching up three horses, Prince, Sally, and a bony dark bay called Captain, Cap for short.

Erik climbed up onto the disk seat and drove to the crossing, drowning the metallic whine of the disk in the creek. As the horses started up the other bank, Prince jerked the ring off the left end of the neckyoke, leaving the right end still attached to Sally's collar. Erik tightened the lines to stop, but the long upper disk tongue, caught in the sagging neckyoke, slammed into Sally's legs. She swerved, jolting Cap into the bushes, and all leaped precipitously forward with the disk. Instantly the wooden disk tongue slipped off the neckyoke.

Thinking the disk was out of control, Erik slid backwards off the seat into the water and lost the lines. The tongue rammed into the ground and broke off at the iron braces. The horses fled wildly up the bank, their traces whipping along the single and doubletree, which yanked the triple tree, and hauled the lurching disk near their heels.

They might yet be stopped by a fence a few yards from the bank, unless Chris had left the gate open. Erik heard an instant crash and then the sickening twang of wires. The disk had smashed against the corner post and ripped out the next post with it, while the horses wheeled left and tore wildly along the fence. Then they lost half of the disk and disappeared in a ravine ahead. Erik instinctively followed the bank to avoid getting trapped against the fence. The horses had come to a stop. Cap was crowded into the fence and had a leg caught in it. Chris was coming, and Erik started running toward the horses.

"Naw!" Chris shouted. He came striding like fate across the field.

Erik stopped until Chris reached the scene, and then Erik followed Chris.

Chris unhooked all of the traces and caught Cap's leg in a vise-like grip to free it from the wire, blood seeping down over Cap's hoof. "Here, hold him!" Chris commanded, as he slapped Cap's lines in Erik's hands. Then Chris moved around in front, and Prince and Sally jumped excitedly. "Whoa," Chris shouted and struck back on their bits. Prince reared, and Chris kicked him savagely in the belly and unleashed pent-up profanity. He turned suddenly on Erik. "How the hell did this happen?"

Erik didn't look up from holding Cap. "The–the neckyoke," he began.

"God a'mighty!" Chris cut in. "Couldn't you see it was busted? D'you expect me to watch you ev'ry damn minute? Look at the goddamn harness and the disk, all shot to hell. Enough to break a man in business." He threw the rest of the lines at Erik. "Git the hell out o' here!"

Prince, Sally, and Cap started off, following Erik, hanging on their lines. Julia stood at the head of the draw and stared stonily at him.

He waited with the horses by the barn door until Chris returned. "Put them in?" Erik said.

"Sure, what d'you think?" Chris noticed Erik's wet legs. "Better git something dry on. Then go ahead and put the grays on the plow."

Chris was bandaging Cap's leg and Julia waiting on him when Erik left. They didn't look up.

The plowed strip looked like a scar in the flat expanse, the upturned gumbo drying in hard lumps. Erik walked up and down behind a moldboard plow drawn by two horses, making long furrows. Alfalfa roots snapped and a heavy band of earth turned before him. After a while he saw Chris drive by in his car, probably after repairs, and Erik watched the shadow creep down the end of the barn. He didn't long for noon to come.

This was wash day, and thankfully Julia wasn't finished when Erik came back for lunch. As Chris hadn't returned yet, Erik ate quickly by himself, his hands tired by the shaking of the plow handles. Then he escaped to the woodshed to wait until it was time to go out again, hoping Chris wouldn't come home before then. Erik draped his wet socks over a piece of baling wire across the top of his north window. He watched Julia putting wash on the lines, the many-colored pieces hanging motionless against the breaks. When he returned to the barn, the strong smell of Lysol wafted from Cap's stall, and Erik saw the hay in Cap's manger remained untouched.

Feeling guilty, Erik returned to plowing the field, and the long afternoon ahead. He tortured his mind reliving the frightful moments of the runaway. If only he had held on to the lines. His one impulse had been to get away from the disk.

He had fled, as he had to admit he'd done with every problem in his life. He'd escaped his father's expectations, the awkward intimacy of his new stepmother and her children, and the trap of their desolate farm. He'd abandoned his own dream when he gave up on his inadequate efforts to become an artist. And finally, in his search for himself, he'd fled his very homeland. Yet now, less than a week here, he had already thought about leaving again.

He didn't see the car return, but at length he noticed Chris had crossed the creek with his hayrack. He had probably seen his father uptown. Then Al would know and everybody. It might get in the paper. As the afternoon wore on, Erik dreaded meeting up again with the family. Louise rode past the end of the field, on her way home from school, and waved to him. He watched her ride on. She would stop and talk with her father, and then she would know.

Chris returned when the sun had nearly reached the horizon. Only then Erik went through the process of unhitching. After he put away their harnesses, cleaned stalls, watered, and put the grays away, Erik came back out, and saw the disk, reassembled with a new tongue, pulled up to the gate for the cornfield. Chris became furious when anything went wrong, but lost no time restoring order. From the yard, Erik could hear Chris feeding the hogs. It would be late before they finished the chores. So much the better.

While Erik groomed the grays, Chris came in. "Pull it all right?" He stepped up beside the horses to check their shoulders.

"Yes."

"Yeah, got to be careful not to get 'em galled. Hard to heal." This obvious advice galled Erik. But Chris added that his brother Al would loan him a horse until they had all the wheat in. "Gonna bring it over tomorrow night." Chris glanced up at Erik. "He thought maybe he'd come early enough to take you up to see Jes's place if you want to."

Erik hesitated.

"Might as well," Chris said. "And in that case, we'd better treat the wheat after supper tonight. Let's go in and eat."

Although not feeling very hungry, Erik followed Chris into dinner.

After dinner, Erik poured formaldehyde solution from a sprinkler while Chris scooped wheat to the other side of the bin. It felt like a ritual in the yellow light of the lantern– the broken phrases, the chant of the scoop, the swish of the grain. Chris took up a handful and let the grains trickle back. "Yeah, that's pretty good," he said almost reverently. Erik smelled a heavy odor, almost like incense.

Al and Erik turned their horses west on the section lane, which led up over the north end of the knolls. The basin already darkened. They passed the farmstead Erik had seen from the road the night he'd arrived.

"Mat Burk's place," Al said. "Used to be purdy nice till the damn water got on it. Now it's all alkali. By golly, you'd think it had snowed. I don't know why the devil he stays on it. Plenty o' places to rent if it's farmin' he wants."

Al talked almost continuously in Danish, and Erik felt a little uncomfortable with him. This hurt, as Erik realized it came from his own inability to talk easily with others, in any language.

Al looked at Erik. "You feelin' all right?"

"Sure." Erik swallowed.

"If it's that runaway that's ridin' you, forget it," Al said. "You couldn't help it. Damn lucky you didn't git run over by the disk. I told Chris. You darn right. He gits himself all worked up and flies off the handle. Don't pay no attention to him."

Erik smiled feebly. He didn't feel ready to forgive himself yet.

The section lane ran straight ahead with fences on both sides, and their ponies walked side by side in the wagon tracks. Erik rode Brownie, Louise's gentle pony. She had insisted. Another expression of sympathy after the runaway. For a while Erik could hear only hoofbeats on the earth, the solid earth, stretching on and on into evening. A thin cold light shone on the plateau.

"Naw," Al began again, "this country ain't no good for farmin'. Look at this damn ditch here cuttin' the side o' the bluffs all to hell. It used to be the purdiest grassland in the Black Hills. You could ride all over the country—no fences, no ditches, no nothin', not even a road, by golly. Makes a feller sick. Costs a hell-of-a-lot of money, too, let me tell you, a darn sight more 'n they'll ever git out of it.

"And that ain't all. Nosiree! It's gonna change people. Look at what it's doin' to Chris or this poor devil up here. Used to be a purdy good guy when he first come over."

A startled rabbit appeared beside them and leaped ahead up the road.

"Hey!" Al shouted, and the rabbit stopped momentarily on its haunches, perked up its long ears, and fled again. "Darn graceful, jumpin' like that. It don't hardly seem to be touchin' the ground. Used to be some antelopes too, and still is out north. 'Course they're gettin' scarcer every year. The damn honyockers shoot 'em, and o' course the coyotes get 'em too."

Honyockers? A word Al had no Danish for, Erik silently guessed.

Al suddenly pulled off onto a trail to the left. The river valley came into view. Al peered ahead as if to get his bearings and altered their course a little westward. Then they saw the slim posts and sagging wires of a fence.

"That's it. It's down in the draw aways." Al rode on toward the fence.

"Is there a gate here?" Erik couldn't see it.

"Naw, we'll have to take the fence down." Al dismounted and pulled out a claw hammer from one of his saddle bags. "A feller's got to carry his tools with him in this country. Can't never tell when he'll need 'em." He loosened the wires at one of the posts and stapled them close to the ground. Then, standing on them, he called to his pony and it walked across. Erik's pony followed, and Al replaced the wires. It wouldn't have been so easy, Erik thought, if the wires had been strung as tight as Chris's new fence.

The descent suddenly became abrupt. Erik pulled on his reins to keep Brownie from running down, and he gripped his saddle horn to keep from sliding into it. Brownie grunted as he sidled down the slope.

"By golly," Al said, "we'll hafto watch out we don't bust in his roof."

And then Erik saw the dugout projecting from the hillside like a dormer window.

Al rode his horse toward the corral, near the bottom of the draw. "Hope he's home. Milkin' maybe."

With relief, at last Erik dismounted Louise's pony. His legs felt like they no longer belonged to him. The door of the cowshed opened and Jes appeared with a milk pail in each hand.

"Hi," Al called.

"Hi." Jes set his pails down. "T'ought I heard somebody." He pushed the door closed and shoved a forkful of manure against it.

Al chuckled. "Purdy handy latch you got there, Jes."

"Ya, I ain't had time to get t'ings fixed up." Jes smiled weakly, showing his bad teeth. "Just gonna let the cows out." He wore a dairyman's long coat, once white but now stained and plastered with milk and manure. The tail ends flapped against his overalls. Al followed him to the gate of the corral, and Erik trailed behind with Brownie.

"Purdy fair bunch, Jes," Al said, as Jes herded his last cows from the cowshed into the corral with the rest.

"You bet. Fifty dollars a head."

"Fifty bucks!" Al exclaimed.

"Ya, I git it back purdy quick." Jes walked into the corral to shoo his herd and a last straggler out. "You can put de horses in dere."

"Turn out the cows nights?"

"Ya, dem stays in de draw."

"Any feed for them down there?"

"Naw, not dat mounts to any t'ing. Dey rustles a little." Jes coughed. "Hay's too dam' high." He unbelted the long coat and shed it, along with his jacket inside it, and hung both on a nail outside the cowshed. "Purdy handy outfit."

Outside the door to his dugout, Jes picked up a stick and scraped the dung from his shoes.

Al stooped to get through the doorway, and Erik followed. The small room smelled musty and stale, like a potato cellar.

Jes lit a kerosene lamp. "Sit down, fellers. I'm gonna make some coffee."

"Naw, don't bother, Jes," Al protested. "Just dropped by for a moment to say 'Hello,' and show the boy where you live." He sat down on a cot along the wall. Erik sat down on the edge of it with him.

"Won't take long," Jes insisted. "Got ever't'ing on de table just about." It was littered with unwashed dishes, part of a loaf of bread, and some butter that had melted and then congealed.

"Not tonight, Jes, thanks," Al said firmly. "Some other time."

Jes shook the grate, and ashes sifted out through the vent. "Guess the dam' fire went out." He squatted on a stool by the stove, coughed hard, and spat in the wood box. "Ya, dis is a hell-of-a-life," he said finally.

"Yeah, you need a wife," Al replied.

"You bet. You too."

"Sure," Al said. "Show me the gal. That's the trouble with a new country, darn few women."

"Vel, I got one dere behind you fellers."

Al and Erik twisted on the cot to look at a picture on the back wall near the foot of the cot. They saw a long glossy print of a smiling girl standing beside a cream separator in a lush meadow.

"Yeah," Al said. "They don't hafto be that purdy. Just a girl. That's good enough for this country. A little softness to take the hardness out o' things."

"You bet," Jes said.

A pause happened like a moment of silent prayer, and then Al turned to Erik. "Well, you think we better git movin' along?" He rose to go.

"I wish I'd knowed you fellers was comin'." Jes followed them out. He stuck close to Al, and they talked for quite a while.

"Gonna prove this claim soon?" Erik heard Al asking Jes.

"Naw. I got to build more. De dugout ain't big enough, Godamit'."

"Hard to git away from the poor devil," Al said to Erik, as they started along the draw on their ponies. They were riding home by way of the Maylands and town, where their roads would part.

Erik's eyes were getting used to the darkness. The draw took a southeasterly direction, the sides steep and blending into the mound-like slopes he had seen from the train.

Al chuckled. "If that don't beat hell, wearin' a long coat like some highfalutin' dairyman. A bit shot, huh? Wonder where he got it. By golly, as dirty as if he'd slept in the manure pile."

"Yes," Erik said, "I don't see how he can stand it."

"Well, sir, you'd be surprised how many do it. Take Gus, he ain't doing a hell-of-a-lot better. They ain't ever had nothin', of course. Gittin' a hundred and sixty acres free they think they got the world by the tail. But, by golly, it takes work to make a livin' out o' the raw prairie."

They could now see the elevated train tracks, the fence along the right-of-way, and the telegraph poles–thin lines to civilization. Al dismounted to open the gate. Erik could still see the light from Jes's dugout, and then it passed from sight behind the slope. They came next to a crossing. The pulsating hum of the telegraph wires seemed infinitely lonely. Their ponies stepped gingerly across the cattle guard, and then quickened into a jog-trot on the narrow road toward the dark trees of Mayland's ranch.

3

Erik walked behind the plow again, east and west along the furrow. The gumbo broke in lumps over the moldboard and jerked the plow handles. Sally stopped on the slightest provocation. Shade crept imperceptibly down the end of the barn, and the afternoon shadows took forever to fill the hollows on the divide.

Then the wind came up from the south, eddying in the flanks of the horses and driving Russian thistles into the fences. Erik's neck grew stiff, keeping his cap on, at an angle to the wind. The lines cut his waist as if they were tied on. He peered dry-eyed up the knolls toward the windswept sun and back to the divide.

At night in the woodshed he felt besieged by the wind. He pulled his dead musty covers up over his head to shut out the sound, and then lay there listening for it. The next morning he felt as if he had fought it all night. With the whining outside, the creak of the shack, and the rattle of windows in his ears, he looked out to make sure it was as bad as ever, and the divide still loomed like a dried brain.

"Yeah," Chris said without feeling later, "you have to expect it this time o' year."

Finally one evening a black cloud bank appeared in the west.

"You can't tell," Chris said. "Sometimes all we get is more wind." But he went outside to connect the rainspout with the cistern.

The cloud rose steadily and spread toward the north. Suddenly a white spear plummeted down its side. Then another and another, and at last came distant thunder.

Wind slapped the screen door back as Erik entered the woodshed. It was not the fitful gust of previous days but a straight blast from the west. He sat down on his bed to wait. Why hadn't they invited him to stay in the kitchen until the storm ended? A blinding light flashed, followed by an instant crash, and the floor shook. A few heavy drops beat on the roof, then wind and rain smashed against the shack. He clung to the edge of the bed, and tried to close his senses to the cloudy deluge spending itself over the divide.

Dripping began at the foot of the bed, slowly at first, then faster. But the thunder was already receding, and soon he noticed there was no longer a light in the kitchen.

"You should have come over to the house by rights," Chris said the next morning. "I wouldn't trust that old shed too far."

"No?"

"No. Not in a storm like that."

Was Chris belatedly trying to make up for not having thought to ask Erik inside his house?

"A dandy rain," Chris added.

The gumbo caked everyone's shoes, but the sky arched high and infinitely blue, and the Black Hills had a fresh, clean-washed look. Louise came to breakfast in a thin, sleeveless dress. How pale her arms looked. And how beautiful the strange words sounded when she spoke. Erik found himself trying to repeat them when he was alone.

As soon as the plowed field dried on top, Chris was on it with a light harrow, rubbing out the clods. Plowing went easier, the furrows falling in clean slices and filling Erik's nostrils with the smell of spring. Robins appeared in the furrows after the plow, and now and then out of the weeds came the flute-like notes of meadowlarks.

Suddenly the divide had a greenish cast. Then one evening the cottonwoods along the creek stood tipped with yellow, as if a giant painter had danced his brush lightly over their tops. Fred was the first to notice them. He had come with Al to dehorn and brand cattle, before taking the herd out north on the range for the summer.

Erik had met Fred once before when he came by to take Louise to a dance. Al had adopted Fred as a boy when his mother died. She had moved from back East, supposedly for her health, and taught a country school near Al's place. Al had expected to keep Fred only until they could get in touch with his relatives. But no one in Fred's family had shown any concern, adding fuel to the rumor that his mother had never married.

Fred slept in the woodshed with Erik and promptly began to help him with his English, repeating words and correcting his pronunciation. Fred hadn't come from a teacher's family for nothing, he declared. Though as for Al, Fred shook his head.

"No use. Al goes through language the way he goes through the country, any way he can. Rules got no more chance than a fence. Sometimes I think he's going to change me instead. He talks so darn much. And he's a lot like the country, if you know what I mean."

Erik thought he did.

"You like this country?"

Erik hesitated, trying to think of what to say and how to say it.

"Maybe you haven't been here long enough to know," Fred came to his aid. "They tell me you used to paint pictures in the old country."

"A little."

"Why don't you keep it up?"

"Oh, I don't know." That was one of the first expressions Erik had learned, and he tried it out now. It seemed to have so many uses.

"You have a little spare time, I guess," Fred persisted. "Sundays anyway. If you didn't bring your stuff to work with, you can get some easy enough. Send away for it anyway. Have Louise or Julia do it."

"I don't know," Erik repeated, pained. It wasn't so simple. How could he put it into words? He had not only abandoned the means but also his will. He hadn't exactly lost interest, but rather he had decided to give up painting as outside his reach. In time he hoped to forget about it. Meanwhile, he didn't want to talk about it. He couldn't talk about it. He shook his head. "I guess not."

"O' course there isn't much around here to paint, I expect," Fred said. "Now out north it's different. You can see the swells of the prairie for miles, with only the blue sky on them. I don't know if anybody has ever painted them. Of course, a photograph can't do anything with them. Julia paints a little, you know. Pretty nice pictures too, but she likes the Hills better, waterfalls and things like that, or just flowers. Maybe the prairies are too big to paint, but anyway you ought to at least go see them."

Erik said he would like to.

"A feller from the university was out there for a while last summer, making some kind of study," Fred continued. "He told me this whole country was once a big inland sea. And I guess that's so. You can find petrified fish out there, scales on them and everything. He said there wasn't even any Black Hills then. It don't seem reasonable. But that was millions of years ago, I guess." He paused. "The son-of-a-gun was trying to get my girl."

"Oh?" Erik said.

"I hope she's still out there. I guess she is. Haven't heard from her for quite a while."

"Oh, out on the prairie?"

"Sure. Where did you think?"

"I didn't think anybody lived out there." Erik said.

"Oh yes. A few. Her family has a homestead out there." Erik nodded uncertainly.

"Oh, I wouldn't blame her," Fred added. "He's a nice feller all right. Different you know from cowhands hanging around there all the time. I s'pose he's been writing to her right along. In fact, I know he has. My friend Bates, the mailman, told me."

"Purdy?"

Fred reached for his billfold and took out a snapshot.

"Yes." Erik nodded over the photo, to cover his confusion. "I see." She was a young woman with a Mona Lisa face.

"She's smart too," Fred said.

"'R. N.'" Erik read in the lower margin.

"Rita. Rita Nicolini."

"Known her long?" Erik said.

"Quite a while. Since the first summer I spent out there."

Why then did Fred take Louise to a dance? But Erik was pleased at how well he had managed to use English, when there was no one around who understood Danish and made him feel self-conscious. And to find out Louise was not yet spoken for. . . .

Fred put his picture away. "Well, I'll see Rita purdy soon. Maybe that's why she hasn't written."

"Yes," Erik said quickly, hoping it was true.

It rained again, and the frogs croaked in the creek at night. Now irrigation ditches had to be cleaned or burned out and new ones made, raw and tortuous gashes in the grainfields. The men struggled and stumbled with their horses in the heavy gumbo. They guessed at the contours and looked back with misgivings. Nerves grew tight and frayed. And after hard days in the fields, next came the unending chores of cleaning stalls, grooming, watering, feeding, and milking in the corral–lashing tails, a sudden kick, and quick dive into the barn to escape the flies.

The alfalfa grew from young green to purple, and the men started cutting. It was a relief to sit on the mower, riding around and around and watching the alfalfa drop quivering over the sickle bar. Erik could hum to his heart's content along with the purr of the mower, without anyone overhearing.

But in the mornings and evenings and when there was no wind, the mosquitoes rose fiercely and stuck thick and bloated along the bellies of the horses. The men wore gloves and draped bandannas from the backs of their hats. Erik slapped at his legs, one side and then the other, staining his overalls. In the evenings he lay scratching in the woodshed, and listened to mosquitoes hitting the screen door and whining over his face, along with the incessant wave-like chorus of the frogs, as if the very creek bottoms had come alive.

Gus arrived to help with stacking. He was fleshy, red-faced, and spoke with a strong Swedish accent, showing his gold teeth. His land joined Chris's on the lower bottoms. Gus lived alone in a sod house he had built himself. Rumors claimed he planned a trip to the old country in the fall to find a wife.

To Erik's delighted surprise, Louise, in brand new overalls, came along to drive the stacker team. Erik drove one of the hay sweeps in the field, so except when he pushed one of his loads onto the stacker, his contacts with her were few. But he made the most of one opportunity. They kept the water jug, in a soaked gunnysack jacket, in a ditch. Erik usually volunteered to retrieve it. Gus called it the "yug." But before Erik tossed it up to him, he always offered it to Louise first and then drank after her, from the exact same spot where her mouth had touched.

"Tastes good," she said.

Only later he wondered if she meant that as a question.

After the alfalfa, they moved on to the wild hay growing on the lower bottom. As it was now too far to go home at noon, they took lunch along, which they ate in the shade of the stack. They didn't talk much except for the usual remarks about the progress of their work, and Louise paid no attention. Instead she found articles to read in the newspaper wrappings of their sandwiches. Erik felt content just to sit beside her in the tangy fragrance of the new hay, and to feel her nearness. He had found it difficult to reconcile her with this bleak country, but it was not so hard now here in the prairie hay. He noticed the tiny light hairs on her forearm, which was browning in the sun.

"Some purdy good hay across the crick, too, Chris," Gus said one day as they finished lunch.

"I expect. I ain't been over there lately."

"You bet." After a pause Gus added, "I vonder somebody don't file on it."

"Yeah," Chris drawled, getting ready to stretch out for his usual nap. "Wouldn't be bad if there was a bridge."

"You bet."

Chris lay with his hat over his eyes.

Gus turned his attention to Erik. "Vy don't you take it?" And noticing Erik's puzzled look, he added, "The homestead over there cross the crick."

"Homestead?"

"Sure," Gus said. "Right next to mine."

Louise looked up.

Gus turned to her. "I t'ought Fred was gonna take it vonce."

"I don't know," she said. "I guess he thought about it." She seemed about to return to her reading, but folded her paper up instead. "Maybe I'll take it."

Both Gus and Erik looked at her.

"What's so funny about that?"

Gus shook his head. "Not'ing."

"Lots o' girls do."

"Sure t'ing."

She rose suddenly. "I think I'll run over and look." She turned to Erik. "You want to come along?"

"Sure." He glanced at Chris.

"I tell him," Gus said, "if he vakes up."

This was Erik's first opportunity to walk alone with Louise. He discovered she was a fast walker, especially when she had a particular destination in mind.

"He was thinking of filing on it at one time," she said. "Fred, I mean. Even picked out a place for the shack."

They squeezed through a fence between the wires, and Louise got her overalls caught. As Erik helped to unhook her, she looked back over her shoulder at him. "Maybe you want it? The homestead, I mean. It's about the last one left around here."

"No." He shook his head. "I don't think so."

They followed an irrigation ditch, which led straight to a flume which crossed the creek. The flume was a spidery, red-painted wooden structure, supporting a line of planks above a galvanized trough.

Louise turned to Erik. "You think you can walk across?"

"Sure. I guess so."

"Some can't." Louise stepped up on the plank footbridge and walked ahead, light and sure, the leafy shadows of a cottonwood on the bank running down her back.

The bushes on the creek bank sank below Erik as he followed, and he paused and started again. If only he had something to hold on to or to touch up here. He dropped to his knees and began to crawl–across one plank, and then one more. Louise glanced back, surprised, and then sat down to watch him. At last the other bank came up and he stood up with it.

Louise rested on almost the last plank, with her feet in the trough. "If it had water in it, I'd take my shoes off and splash."

They almost seemed to have forgotten what they'd come for. She looked up at him. "Forget it," she said. "There's a fallen cottonwood up the crick a little ways we can cross back on."

Forget it. It felt like an echo. Al had said it about the runaway the night they rode to Jes's. Erik already had so much to forget.

Louise swiveled around, leaned back, lifted her feet to the last plank, and rose in a single fluid motion like a dancer. She pointed toward the divide. "I guess that's the place he was thinking of."

Erik didn't see. He was looking at her.

She turned her head quickly. "Don't you think?"

He nodded dumbly and followed her along the bank, winding in and out among clumps of sagebrush, and watched her legs swishing in the tall needle grass.

She bent over a clump of sagebrush. "Smells good, doesn't it?" Her hair was the color of the sun amongst silvered twigs.

"Does it?"

"Sure." She pulled on a stalk, letting it slip through her hand, and then held her palm up to him. "Smell for yourself."

He put his face to it.

"Sagebrush perfume," she said, laughing.

"Sagebrush," he repeated to himself. "Sagebrush!" How good it sounded when she said it–full-throated with the rush of her breath, clean outdoor breath, the breath of meadows and wild hay.

Erik had to help Gus in turn with his hay, and they ate their noon meal together in his sod house. Gus had planted hollyhocks by his door, but he was no housekeeper. It looked as if he never made his bed or washed his sheets.

"It alvays stays nice and cool in de summer and varm in de vinter," Gus said, as he started the fire in his stove their first day. "I don't know vy dey don't build more houses like dis in dis country."

Gus picked up a can of Campbell's baked beans. His hands were fat and woolly. "But de bach'ing ain't no good."

"No?"

"No." Gus jacked the can opener. "I had enough."

Erik nodded.

"Fifteen years now." The top of the can dropped down, and fishing it out, Gus stuck his dirty fingers in the beans.

"That long?" Erik said.

"You bet." Gus licked his fingers. "I t'ank I git married."

"You know somebody?"

Gus shook his head. "I go to de old country and find von."

"Coming back?"

"Sure t'ing." He shook the beans out in a pan. "You want to rent my place?"

"Me?"

"Vy not?"

Erik forced a laugh. "You can't mean it." He hardly knew what he was doing here yet.

"Sure t'ing," Gus insisted.

Erik couldn't help feeling flattered, but he shook his head. "No, I don't think so."

"Vel, you t'ank it over. You git half the crop."

In the days that followed, the idea kept coming back to Erik. The unclaimed homestead also beckoned across the creek. But moving into Gus's lair, sleeping in his bed, the lonely Sundays down here!

Erik felt relieved when he returned to work at Chris's and began cultivating the corn. He rode up and down the rows, over flecked leaves and pungent smells. The windy days of plowing felt so far away now. Erik's thoughts returned again and again to the homestead across the creek, especially when morning lay translucent on the cornfield and the meadow.

But his desire ebbed with the day, as he remembered it had also done back home. The sunlight from the west always had such a lonely feel, like the loneliness in the wail of the afternoon train coming down the flats.

The dry weather hung on, and Erik had to help irrigate the grainfields. Water poured from the sluices, spread through the laterals over parched ground, and seethed and bubbled in the cracks. Erik advanced with the water. Dams had to be made in low places and channels cut. He crossed and recrossed the field, dragging his hot rubber boots and bogging down the grain as he went. When he stopped to dig, the gumbo sucked in his boots and stuck to his shovel, and he gazed wearily over the sultry field.

He had to return after supper in the half-darkness to the ditches, rank and cloying with sweet clover and thick with mosquitoes. And after leaving the water for the night, with only the vaguest notion of where it had been or where it would go, he made his way home in his plopping boots, with his shovel first on one tired shoulder and then the other, and the pulsating cries of the frogs behind him. He walked straight to the woodshed and, exhausted, furiously brushed mosquitoes from the screen door.

After a few days the color of the grain showed where the water had run, where it had not gone, and where it had stood too long. And the work went into another cycle: the second cutting of alfalfa, more irrigating, helping Gus again. And the wheat ripened. Erik recalled the night he and Chris had treated the seed by lantern light–the night of the runaway. After all the work and fretful hours along the ditches, the big yellow field grew to meet the sky, the wind running through it all.

Gus came again, to help with the shocking, and though they were not far from the house, they ate in the field to save time.

"Vel," Gus said to Erik one noon, "you t'ought anymore about renting my place yet?"

Erik shook his head.

Gus turned to Chris. "You t'ank you need him dis vinter?"

"Oh, I guess not. Not much to do o' course." He glanced toward Erik. "One trouble is we ain't hardly got room. That damn shed ain't no good when it gets cold. A feller oughta git it tarpapered sometime."

Erik saw Louise coming with the lunch basket and coffee pail.

"Vel, vot you t'ank, Chris?" Gus asked.

"Well." Chris looked from one to the other. "I s'pose it depends on what he wants to do. Wouldn't take a hell-of-a-lot o' work, I guess." He paused. "What's she staring at anyway?" He stood up first, and then the others joined him.

A new car drove slowly down the section lane.

"Al!" Gus exclaimed. "I heard he bought one."

"Yeah," Chris drawled.

They heard Al race the motor for a ditch, and the car leaped over it and came bouncing across the stubble to them. He stopped it with a jerk, still racing the motor.

"You run it too damn fast," Chris called.

"What?"

"You run it too fast when it's idling," Chris said.

"Hell no, you got to," Al shouted, taking his foot off the gas to show his brother. "The sonofagun." Al listened incredulously to the idling motor. "By golly, it won't die when you ain't looking." He turned the switch off and hopped out.

The men drew closer and Louise joined them. Al opened the hood to show off the motor.

"All you need now is a vife," Gus said.

"Yeah," Al agreed. "If this don't help, Gus, I give up. You watch me chase' em down the section lanes."

"Just so you stay on the lanes," Chris warned. "It ain't like a saddle horse, you know."

"By golly, I'll git it broken."

"That's what I was thinking."

Al laughed with them. "That's right. I guess you can't use horse language on a car, can you?" He turned to Erik. "Wonder if you fellers could spare a drink."

"Sure." Erik left to fetch the jug from the ditch, and returned with water dripping from the gunnysack cover.

"Got a diaper on it, I see," Al said.

"Bathing suit," Louise corrected.

"That so?" Al gulped water and looked back at her. "What is it, honey, a boy or a girl?"

A loud blare issued from the horn–Gus trying it out. "You bet," he said, facing them.

When their laughter subsided, Al handed the jug back to Erik and turned to Chris. "Well, what I came for was to see if you could spare the boy a week or ten days. We got that damn fence to put up out north. Fred's gittin' kinda in a hurry about it."

"I s'pose so," Chris replied. "After we git through here."

They turned to go back to work, and Erik, seeing Louise depart, hurried alongside her.

"Looks like you're going on a trip," she said. "I wish I was a boy. I never get to go any place. Darn it."

He shifted the jug to his other hand. He wanted to touch her, or say something. But they had already reached the ditch where the jug was kept, and he could only stand there and watch her go, her swift legs moving in the seed-heavy grass. She didn't look back.

4

Al had hitched four horses to his load. On top of posts he'd stacked reels of wire, a few bales of hay and sacks of oats, cartons with groceries, and some tools. He'd tied Cap on behind for Erik.

"I feel better already," Al said, when they'd crossed the divide. They passed a well-kept ranch with a red barn. "Steve's place. You won't see any more like that on this trip." Al began to point out the landmarks ahead: Broken Rock, Twin Buttes, and Saddle Horn farther east. "We go right by Broken Rock."

"Today?"

"Naw, hell no, not today. It's forty miles, I expect." Al peered at Erik. "You ain't gettin' tired already?"

"No."

"Naw, I hope not." After a pause, Al said, "This ain't nothin' compared with early days. When we first came to this country, we was on the road two, three weeks. Pa, he met us in Fort Pierre. That was as far as the train went in them days. He had come ahead, you know, a couple years before, to find a place and git it fixed up. Well, he had a covered wagon, all right, one he'd borrowed, I guess, and a couple old plugs. We camped just any place there was water, a crick or water hole of some kind.

"One morning the horses was gone, and Pa and Chris went looking for 'em. It gives you a god-awful feeling to be left like that on the prairie, miles and miles from any place. It was kinda misty and raw. Ma just sat there and cried. I was about eight, I guess, something like that. That was the time some Indians came. Ma tried to give 'em potatoes, but they wouldn't have 'em. And after a while they left."

Al paused. "I can still see 'em riding up the draw. There was three of 'em. Long black hair like manes. One of 'em old and wrinkled. I don't know if they could talk English. They sure as hell couldn't talk Dane, which was all Ma knew. I guess they soon found out they'd come to the wrong party. Maybe they'd seen our horses and just come to tell us about that."

"Did you find them?"

"Oh yeah. After a while Pa and Chris came riding back on 'em. We was sure tickled to see 'em. That's about all I remember except the night we first seen Bear Butte. Pa said we could see home. And when we got there it was only a dugout. The funny part is Ma gits kinda homesick for it once in a while. I guess it's where people suffer most that they git attached.

"You can imagine what it was like," Al continued. "No furniture, only what Pa made, and he ain't no carpenter by a long shot. The stove--I hope it's in hell, it smoked like the devil. I remember one winter we was snowed in, Ma ground corn for bread in our coffee mill.

"Talk about hard times. I don't know if she told you. Our little sister, she died out there. Took a bad cold and it turned to pneumonia. 'Course, the folks didn't know what it was till too late. No doctor handy or anything. Only three, four years old, the purdiest kid you ever seen.

"Course, after we moved over on the river, it was a little better. We was in a log cabin for a while. An old sonofagun. Well, it was the first feller that settled over there that put it up.

"Chris tore it down a few years back. Thought he could use the logs for a bridge across the crick. But the damn thing flooded out the next spring. That was before they put in the irrigation dam. Served him right, too. I didn't know nothin' about it till one day I seen him and Gus hauling a load through town. Hell, I'd have bought it and left it. Something of the early days, you know. Chris don't care nothin' about that, seems like. Thinks he's gonna remake the country."

Al stretched out his legs. "Well, sir, he can have his dirty hogs, all pent up and slobbering swill from a trough. And there's another thing. A feller out here ridin' around and lookin' after stock is more decent. Just moseys along, helpin' any critter that's in trouble. I ain't never seen a mean cattleman."

Erik immediately remembered seeing Chris viciously kick Prince in the belly soon after the runaway.

Well past the middle of the day, they finally reached the pond where Al planned to stop for lunch. The pond lay at the foot of a group of three buttes, which from a distance had looked like a bat with its wings outspread. As Erik would return alone on Cap and could make a shortcut to the pond from Broken Rock, Al took special pains to have him notice the location. Al added, "But if the weather's not clear, you'd better stick to the trail and go 'round by Joe's. We're gonna stay there tonight."

After eating they drove on, into the level prairie shimmering with needle grass in the afternoon. Erik sat watching the bobbing heads of the horses and their sturdy, hard-working legs. "Joe," he asked after a while, "does he know we're coming?"

"Naw, I guess not, unless he's seen Fred lately."

"Married?"

"No." Al shook his head. "Just another old bachelor."

Even Al seemed to have talked himself out. They watched a hawk wheeling slowly overhead, around and around, its wings tilting in the sun. Then there was only the great silence of the earth and sky and the sun sinking ever so slowly, turning Broken Rock amber as shadows crept into the draws.

At last Joe's shack rose abruptly beyond the top of a slope, and to the right a shed and corral appeared. Al drove up in front of the shack.

"It don't look like he's home." Al peered around, and then both men got down from Al's wagon. "Naw," Al repeated, "I guess he ain't."

But there was a note and a row of brands at the bottom of it, all scrawled with chalk on the door:

"Dear Friend

If you come here

And we are not Home

Help yourself

To Food and Bed.

P. S. Do you know these Brands?"

Al knocked, then peeked through a window.

"Well," he said, "we'll unhitch and give him a chance."

But Joe didn't show up, and after they put their horses in the corral, they entered the shack and started the stove fire.

"You can git the flour down," Al said to Erik.

The flour sack lay on a board suspended by baling wires from the ceiling.

"To keep the mice out, o' course." Al watched Erik get up on a chair. "Not a bad idea, unless they can slide down the wires, and they'd sure have a heck of a time gittin' back up."

Erik reached for the sack.

"That slab o' bacon too," Al added.

It grew dark inside, and Al lit a lamp. He started whistling but didn't get much out of it. "I wonder," he said suddenly, "if that phonygraph is still runnin'." He wiped his hands. "You finish slicin' them potatoes." Al moved over to the machine and attached the horn. "You know, it's a darn wonder how anybody could figger out a contraption like this." It crackled. "Edison Record!" he said. "You hear that?"

A husky voice began to sing "Red Wing," and Al hummed along with it as he returned to the stove.

"Now, I call that a darn purdy song," he said, when it finished. Then they heard footsteps outside. "You old sonofagun," Al called out. "It's about time."

"Supper ready?" Joe asked as he ducked inside. Al pumped Joe's arm, and Joe glanced past him. "Who's your friend?" His voice was high-pitched and squeaky.

Al introduced Erik but couldn't remember his last name. "Well, a feller don't need no more than one name in this country anyway."

Erik stood to shake Joe's hand.

"Pleased to meet you." Joe was lean, the sun had turned his skin to leather, and his eyes watered. He walked stiffly in his boots across the room, and hung his hat on a nail below a small picture. In the faint light Erik could barely see it, and he couldn't help stepping closer.

"It's a watercolor, isn't it?" he asked Joe.

"I dunno. I got it at a fair once."

Al came over to look. "That's a funny lookin' deer. Green, ain't it?"

"They claim an Indian painted it," Joe said.

"Musta been color-blind," Al said.

"I dunno."

"Maybe he didn't have no other kind o' paint," Al tried again.

"We-ell," Joe squeaked, "maybe that's the way it looked to him. Could be. Sorta got himself in it."

"Oh, it ain't that bad," Al objected.

Joe exchanged puzzled looks with Erik, then asked "You know something about painting?"

"A little." Erik looked away.

"Yeah, he used to be a painter in the old country," Al said.

Joe nodded. "We-ell, I don't know. There ain't much to it, I s'pose. Like something in the first grade."

He went to wash at the basin, and then they were ready to sit down. Al moved the lamp over to the table.

"This is a treat," Joe said. "It don't often happen to me."

"I know what you mean." Al poured the coffee. "We was tryin' out your phonygraph. I guess you heard."

Joe nodded. "Just the same old records, Al."

"That's what I like. Purdy 'Red Wing' and old pieces like that."

"Talkin' about Indians," Joe said, "I seen something on this trip I won't forgit."

"Ye-ah?"

"It was out in the Slim Buttes. I was passin' a tepee and heard somebody groanin' inside. I didn't know if I should go in, so I stayed purdy close and then I found out. It was a young lady Indian havin' a baby by herself."

"No?" Al exclaimed. "You seen it?"

"I sure heard it! Then she came out after a while with the kid and washed it in a water hole."

"Gosh. Left to herself, poor thing. Did she see you?"

"I guess so. She didn't pay no attention, though. Too sick, prob'ly. After a while I left. I s'pose some of her folks musta been around there somewhere."

"Gosh, you'd think so." After a pause, Al continued. "Well, sir, it ain't been so easy for settlers either. I was tellin' the boy here on our way about the tough times my folks had in the early days.

"But it's purdy good country anyway, ain't it, Joe? Purdy good! Seems like home, gittin' out here again, smellin' the prairie all day, and then a good meal like this. I sure like fried potatoes and onions."

"I expect," Joe said, "the reason you like it is you ain't out here much."

"It's just the way it used to be on the river when I was a kid. God's country we used to call it. Now it's out here–just the way He left it when He got through workin' on it."

"You mean," Joe said, "when people move in, God moves out."

"That's about it."

"We-ell, what are you coming out here for then?"

Al smiled. "That's a good question." He looked at Erik. "Ain't it?"

"Or maybe you ain't the kind God moves out on?" Joe prompted.

"Hell no! We're on the same side. Damn tired of being all fenced in, irrigated, and mosquito-bitten."

"Yeah?" Joe led Al on.

"You darn right."

"What are you bringing a fence for then?"

Al hesitated a moment. "That's another good question." Al turned to Erik again. "Ain't it?"

"I'm waiting," Joe squeaked.

"You're waiting. That's fine. Just fine, you old coyote. I thought you were a friend o' mine."

"Or was you just gonna sneak a load out o' the country to git rid of it?" Joe suggested.

"That's it. Why couldn't I think of that?"

"We-ell," Joe said, "you're too busy back on the river to think. And I ain't busy enough not to. But it don't make no difference. We just go 'round and 'round like a wagon wheel. And when it stops it's still a wagon wheel."

"Yeah," Al agreed. "Why don't you start that phonygraph going 'round and 'round while we empty the coffee pot?"

"Sure." Joe got up and wound the spring.

"Yeah," Al drawled, "that's what I should have bought instead of a piano."

"You got a piano?" Joe asked incredulously.

"Damn right."

"What the devil you want that for?"

"Oh, some darn fool talked me into it."

Joe exchanged glances with Erik again.

"Oh, the piano is all right," Al said defiantly. "A baby grand, by golly. I don't know why a baby. It's as big as . . ." he looked around. "Well, you ain't got anything that big around here. But you've seen 'em. Kinda like a big three-legged milk stool." He paused. "The only trouble is there ain't nobody to play it."

Joe picked out a record and pressed it on the cylinder. "This is a lullaby for zoo animals, lonesome for their old home in the jungle."

A woman's voice sang, clear and tender except for the scratches and crackles. Erik had trouble understanding the song, but its refrain went something like this:

"Goodnight, Mr. Elephant
Goodnight, Kangaroo
When another day is breaking
All of you will be awaking
In the zoo
In the zoo."

After their first day of fencing, Al, Erik, and Fred relaxed on the steps of Fred's shack. Then Al remembered to tell Fred about the young Indian mother Joe had seen in the Slim Buttes.

"That's the trouble in this country," Al said. "You're out o' luck if you need help quick. Take Joe now. If he got sick, he'd lay there and die more'n likely before anybody'd find 'im. Some git caught like the two girls you was tellin' about."

"You bet," Fred said.

"Tell Erik about it."

"Oh, it was a couple girls out in the Cave Hills last winter," Fred began.

"Over that way." Al pointed northwest.

"One of 'em had a claim out there," Fred continued. "She was a school teacher, so she could only stay there on vacations. Just putting in enough time to hold her claim. So she was going to spend Christmas vacation there, and her sister went along for company–just a kid. They got a ride with a feller that was driving through. It was a kinda warm day."

"That's the kind you hafto watch out for," Al warned. "It'll change on you just like that. I remember one time we was coming home from the Hills. . . ." He broke off. "You go ahead."

"Well," Fred said, "they hadn't more than got there till it turned cold like the dickens and started snowing–a regular blizzard. Nobody could get through for days. When their folks finally reached the shack, the girls were both dead– frozen stiff in bed. They'd forgot to bring matches."

"I don't know what the devil that feller was thinking about," Al exclaimed. "Lettin' them kids off and not going in to see if everything was all right."

Al fell silent for a moment as the sun began to set. Broken Rock loomed darkly, its flat top level with a strip of stratus cloud caught in the glare. Erik watched the light changing in it, from rose to a brilliant satin and then to a fiery glow on the underside, cooling like a bar on an anvil.

"Purdy, ain't it?" Al said. "I remember the time I was up on Broken Rock. By golly, we came down in a hurry."

"Yeah, I remember you telling about it," Fred said. "Quite a few times."

"Yeah." Al turned to Erik. "You ain't heard it, I guess."

"No."

"Well sir, it's a good many years ago now. We'd stopped along the east side to eat lunch. Chris's family was along, and Louise was runnin' around lookin' for arrowheads. She was just a kid then, and I s'pose we wasn't payin' much attention. Purdy soon we seen her climbing Broken Rock. I don't know if she couldn't hear our shouts, but she was always like that anyway. And when she seen me comin', she just loped up the side. It sure gits you in the knees if you ain't used to it.

"What worried me was a narrow, slippery ledge. You know how it is if you're being followed. She was heading right for it too. She glanced back to see if I was coming, and then kept right on going. I don't know what put it into my head, but I suddenly stopped quick and bent down like I was pickin' up something. And, by golly, right in front o' me was the biggest rattlesnake you've ever seen. Louise stopped all right, thinkin' I'd found an arrowhead, and came running back. Holy gee whiz, there wasn't one snake but a whole nest of 'em!"

"She saw them?" Erik said breathlessly.

"I dunno. I don't know how she missed them. Just plain lucky. We both was. Heh. She was sore because I fooled her about the arrowhead. I remember that."

The cloud had lost its glow, and Broken Rock grew even darker against the evening sky. The moon shone in its first quarter, pale and lonely. Al started humming, and soon Fred joined in with the song:

"And the moon shines tonight
On purdy Red Wing
My purdy Red Wing
So far away."

The stars pricked through. Erik hadn't watched them in a long time. He'd had time only for the earth. Out here time stood still. He wasn't sure what day it was. Probably Al and Fred wouldn't know either without stopping to think, and it would be impertinent to ask them. But after a while, Al began yawning, and they turned in. Erik lay awake a long time, listening to the silence and watching the moon through the screen door. It was curious how the light made a cross on the screen, and he looked at it first with one eye and then the other.

Erik learned fencing was very different out here. No one was in any hurry. It was a temporary fence anyway, with only a single wire, just enough to keep the horses in. Al worked hard in spurts but got easily sidetracked. They stopped to test Fred's discovery that the flower of the yellow cactus would close up when one stuck a finger in it.

"I'll be darned," Al exclaimed, and trotted on to another clump of yellow cacti to repeat the experiment.

"You don't have to try 'em all," Fred called after him.

"Look at this sonofagun," Al piped gleefully. "By George, I have a notion to take a bunch of 'em home."

Erik laughed convulsively.

Fred looked at him. "What's the matter with you?"

Erik shook his head. "I don't know." He felt strangely lighthearted, as he had not felt before in Dakota, perhaps never before. This was more like the Dakota he had vaguely imagined–the sunlit slopes, the soft wind, the smell of the prairie. He repeated the name aloud when he was alone: "Da-ko-ta . . . Dakota." Then hers: "Lou-ise"–round, full, and soft in a whisper.

They came to a petrified log on the side of a gully. Fred bent over one end of it. "See the tree rings. When I first saw it, I thought it was real."

Erik ran a hand along the side. "Pine, isn't it?"

"Sure."

"They don't grow here now?"

"No," Fred said. "You have to get into the Hills to find pines. The climate must have been a lot different. There's petrified wood all around this part of the country. They say this was once an inland sea. I s'pose there must have been woods here before that. God only knows what it was like."

Erik looked back at the silent stone witness. It came out of a distant age with the same nature as now–the same grain and knots, the browns and amber of earth and sun. Nature made the only real art. And he saw himself striding around the homestead across the creek, his hammer blows ringing along the wire, as he fenced himself in. He could turn prairies into large framed canvases.

When they had only a day's work left, Al decided to ride over to the Moreau River. "On business," he declared.

"He's just tired of fencin' if you ask me," Fred said, when he and Erik ate supper alone that evening. "I'm getting kind of fed up with it myself. Aren't you?"

"I don't know."

"You like it out here?" Fred asked.

"I don't know if I would all the time," Erik said.

Sunlight paled on the sod outside the door, and the tiny dry grass spears pointed their shadows toward it.

"This country grows on you." Fred nodded. "You can go in any direction and not butt into somebody's fence or ditch all the time. A feller naturally feels freer, like he was somebody. And he doesn't have to work like the devil. He can take a day off when he feels like it and no sonofagun to make you feel like a shirk."

"But doesn't it get lonesome?" Erik asked again, barely hinting at his own feelings: his long Sundays, the windblown prairie in the sun, the bleak voice of the wind on his screen door, and then, suddenly, the blackness in the west splitting with lightning and rain smashing over the land.

"It depends," Fred said. "If you have a nice place and your girl, you'd think this was heaven."

The window behind Fred dulled to slate. It had Al's brand scrawled on it.

"In the spring o' the year you ought to see it out here," Fred continued. "Wild flowers galore, whole yellow slopes of 'em. And now, with fall coming on, the prairie will be like a carpet of color."

He and Erik washed dishes in silence. "Seems kinda quiet with Al gone," Fred said at last. "It's a relief too in a way." They both laughed. "What d'you say we go down and take a dip in the pond before we turn in?"

It wasn't deep enough to swim in, but it was cool. They splashed each other in the moonlight, all naked as if they were alone on the earth. And when they lay in bed, the air flowed in from the draw over their outstretched bodies, while the moon filled the night with silver.

Cap grunted as he moved into a trot again, blowing his feelings out through his nostrils. He was definitely rough, the motions from his long stiff legs hitting the saddle like pistons. Erik couldn't get his ups and downs properly timed, and he compromised by standing up in the stirrups. He shifted his weight tiredly from one stirrup to the other. It was getting hot, too. He still had a long ride to the bat-shaped buttes and their pond.

He spotted a sheep wagon by itself off to the west. In the immense plain it looked like a toy wagon a boy had left behind, to take his toy sheep out to graze. Erik thought of Fred, alone again out there. They had parted along the trail to Broken Rock, Fred to ride out where the herd was, out where morning traveled up the shadowy draws and the sun rose big and red over the rim of the prairie, the rim of the earth. Out where he meant to live with a black-haired girl from the Moreau. Rita! Erik shifted to his other side again. He shouldn't have gone along with Fred out to the cattle yesterday. Too much riding all at once.

Erik lowered his eyes against the sun. A thick, matronly soap weed stood by itself, and beyond it a prairie dog sat yapping by its hole. Others sat bolt upright in a row on their front porches and watched him pass through town. "God's country," Al had called it. One could lose perspective out here. Or find it. With Louise, with her alone here, this might be heaven. With her, Erik could live a simple life on these sunlit slopes, stretching toward the horizon and the Black Hills. They'd live off the good earth, rising out of an ancient sea.

Cap stopped with a jerk. Erik raised his reins to slap him and in the same moment heard a sharp whir. Cap backed up, and Erik yanked on the reins, glancing frantically at a squirming coil on the ground. He just wanted to get away from the rattlesnake, as fast as possible. He could feel his heart pounding, as he peered ahead in the grass.

No one need know that he'd fled, once again. He had nothing to kill it with anyway. Not a thing. He told himself to just look around it, and keep riding toward the buttes and the pond. He was thirsty. His shirt stuck to his back.

Almost against his will Erik glanced to his left. Just a gully. No use looking, and he looked again anyway. All he saw were big, heavy rocks, probably too large and stuck in the ground. Al hadn't said anything about trying to kill rattlers near Broken Rock. Getting off Cap was too dangerous. Especially here, miles and miles from anybody. Cap kept stepping back. Nobody would ever know.

Or should Erik mention it? A rattlesnake got away from him. As a warning. Everyone could be on the lookout. So he wouldn't be to blame if anything happened. They might even get it sometime. He probably couldn't find it now even if he wanted to. If only Al or Fred had come along with him. "Hell, it might kill somebody," Erik could hear Al saying.

Erik studied the gully yet again. Maybe he could hit the snake with a rock from his horse. If the rattler had disappeared by the time he found some good throwing stones, he couldn't help it. At least he would have tried, instead of running away again. They would expect him to try. Louise would expect him to. There was no one else to do it. He alone had spotted it and was responsible. He tightened his lips and pulled again on Cap's reins, this time toward the gully.

Cap resisted at first, turning only his head. So Erik jerked him around, and prodded him with his heals. Erik found suitable rocks in the gully after all, after he dismounted to collect as many as he could fit in his saddle bags, and to carry and pile in front of him on the saddle. Then he rode as close as Cap would go–a few steps.

The rattler still coiled in the same place. It gave another sharp warning, and Erik nervously threw his first rock. But Cap took it as a threat to himself and reared, spilling rocks down his sides. One hit Erik on his ankle, and he bent over it in pain. He couldn't do this. Not from a horse.

He rode back a few yards. His ankle tingled and blood seeped through his sock. He dismounted painfully, tied the saddle rope onto Cap's bridle, and hung onto the rope to keep Cap from bolting. Erik switched the rope from his right to his left hand. He'd taken one rock in each hand from his saddle bags, and let the rope out to allow Cap to stay back. Erik stepped closer this time but missed again, the deadly head flickering over the moving coil. He dived quickly for one of the flat stones dropped from the saddle and hurled it. It fell just short, but the rattler suddenly thrust forward over it. Erik snatched up another rock and struck the snake on the head.

In no hurry now, he nearly buried the snake with rocks before he cut the rattle off with his pocket knife. To take home and show them. His ankle felt worse than it looked. If only he had some water to drink.

Erik finally rode near the buttes after mid-afternoon. They stood round and firm like sunlit breasts of the prairie.

Cap waded right into the pond and muddied the water, and so guzzled first and endlessly. Then Erik drank in another spot, lying flat on his stomach with his hands in the mud. The water was cloudy and warm, and tasted of summer and gumbo. And his sandwiches were dry and warped, but none of it mattered.

Erik sat down on the smooth carpet of buffalo grass, and ate and gazed serenely back over the many miles toward Broken Rock. Its top looked as flat as an altar, and it turned gold in the late afternoon sun.

Later, from the tops of slopes, he could see the Black Hills. A rain cloud hovered over the north end, and as he rode on, the cloud lifted and spread like a benediction. The sun slipped behind it and sank into a mist beyond the Hills, staining the hem of the cloud with crimson.

Then he spotted the farmstead with the red barn he had noticed on the way out. Between the farmstead and the trail, a lone rider waved. Erik cautiously raised his hand. Someone had mistaken him for somebody else as he rode closer. But the other rider waited, a straight figure sitting immobile on a pony. Blood suddenly rushed into Erik's face.

"You didn't recognize me?" Louise said, as he rode up beside her.

"No. I didn't expect you out here."

She took up her reins, and Brownie stepped into the other wheel track. "I came to see if Steve can help thresh."

"Oh? Right now?"

"Day after tomorrow, if it doesn't rain," she said. "Uncle Al isn't coming, I s'pose."

"No. Not right away."

There was a pause.

"Like it out there?" she asked at last.

"Ye-es."

"Joe all right?"

"Yes."

"And Fred?"

"Fine."

"See his girl?"

"No-o."

Louise was looking straight ahead, and Erik studied her face–her straight nose, high cheek bones, and her perfectly modeled chin. His hand made a quick involuntary motion. Thinking with his artist's mind again. He couldn't seem to help it, no matter how hard he tried to forget.

She noticed the gesture but said only, "I guess she's very pretty."

His eyes dropped to her firm breasts jutting against her shirtwaist. "Not as purdy as you," he finally blurted out.

"Ah you," she retorted. "You haven't even seen her."

"I can imagine. I've seen her picture."

"Oh? He showed it to you?"

"Ye-es."

"Out there?"

"No-o. A long time ago."

"Oh?" She fell silent again. Was she startled? Disappointed?

"Why?" he asked, and then wished he hadn't.

"Nothing. Doesn't make any difference to me. He can have all the girls he wants for all I care." She turned toward him almost defiantly. "Can't he?"

Erik didn't answer. This had gone far enough. "I saw a rattlesnake on my way back," he said instead.

"Did you kill it?"

"Sure." He reached into one of his saddle bags and proudly handed her the rattle in a piece of lunch paper. His first trophy.

She opened the paper. "A big one, wasn't it? How did you kill it?"

"With a rock . . . rocks."

She held it out toward him. "Here's your rattle." She laughed. "Sounds funny, doesn't it?"

He didn't understand.

"Rattle," she repeated, shaking it in the paper. "That's what a baby plays with."

"Oh?" Erik's face fell.

After a little she said, "You know something? We're driving up to the Hills some Sunday after we get through threshing."

"Ye-es?"

"I'm going to talk Uncle Al into taking his car so you can come along too. If you want to."

"Yes, I'd like to."

"Grandpa and Grandma will join us too, o' course. They want to go to the cemetery along the way anyway."

He nodded.

"But don't say anything to Papa. I don't think he'll like for Uncle Al to drive in the Hills. Papa thinks he's reckless."

The horses walked close together. Erik could have touched her.

Louise pointed. "See the moon rising over the divide."

"Yes, it's beautiful," he said. Her pale hair glowed in the moonlight.

5

"I don't know how he'd do on them grades." Chris shook his head.

"Al won't have to take his car," Julia said brightly. "We can all go in ours."

"Maybe the boy'd like to go too."

"No, that's all right," Erik spoke up. He knew it was what they wanted him to say. That was why they'd brought it up.

"I suppose somebody should stay," Julia suggested innocently. "On account of the chores, I mean." Chris leaned over to meet his tea, but Julia caught him with her look. "You think we'd get home in time?"

Chris took his time blowing on his tea. "'Course not."

"I didn't think so," she said with her smallest voice.

"Maybe Gus could come up," Chris replied.

"Oh?" Julia glanced at Erik, but he didn't protest.

And that's how it turned out. Erik felt like he was inside one of his own daydreams, sitting beside Louise on the back seat of Chris's car, and riding into the morning freshness, away from the divide and his Sunday loneliness. Her bright skirt fanned out toward him like hope itself.

"You think Al will put us in his back seat?" Erik said. They were going to change to Al's car at Mayland's, so Mayland and Martha could ride with Chris and Julia.

"I expect." Louise put her hand on the seat protectively.

"I was just wondering." Erik looked out his window, and watched corn rows turn like spokes.

"Mr. Hayden is coming too," she said.

"Who?"

"Mr. Hayden. You know, the editor of the paper."

"Oh, him?" After a little Erik added, "He'll want to sit in front, won't he?"

Louise smiled at him. "I expect."

But he didn't. While Erik turned the crank on the front of Al's car, Hayden slipped onto the back seat with Louise. Erik had to sit in front, next to Al.

"By golly," Al said, "it don't make no difference how old a guy gits, he'd rather talk to a girl. You old sonofagun."

Chris glanced at the sound of Al's motor. He was tying a folded canvas chair to the back of his car.

"If you don't catch up," Al called to him, "we'll wait in the cemetery."

Chris nodded and they were off, back toward town and south across the river into dry upland slopes. Hayden laughed. The big stiff, Erik thought resentfully, wondering why Hayden had to come along. It was Al's fault. Always picking up somebody. Then Erik thought of himself, and tried to calm down.

They would soon enter country Erik had passed through his first day here. All that morning his train had skirted the Hills. He'd felt dirty after a long night of sitting up without being able to wash, because the water tank was empty. From his window he'd gazed at last year's stubble and cornfields, dumpy haystacks on creek bottoms, rambling farmsteads, and at last a place to stop–a siding with stock pens.

Erik had wondered about the cornfields. How the stalks could grow in rows every way he looked. And the ears! He had seen a husked corncob in a feed store back home, and had supposed they grew like that on top of stems, like heads of grain. How ignorant and naive.

He had also worried about getting rid of a dried bread crust–what was left of a loaf he had unintentionally bought at the station lunch room in Chicago, where he'd tried to get a meal by pointing at what he wanted.

His train out of New York on his first day had passed through a misty fog, while he wondered what the states to the south looked like, where Lincoln had declared war about fifty years ago to free the slaves. He couldn't imagine living the life of a slave. . . .Meanwhile the train tracks had followed the shore of Lake Erie for hours.

Then he had a long wait in Chicago. He had hoped for clear daylight by the time his train reached the Mississippi, and he had seen it under a silver sky, the great muddy river flowing down the face of America.

America. What indescribable feelings it had aroused! Very deep feelings. Feelings of leaving home, perhaps never to return. "Amerika," as a Dane would say. Always seriously. No one would ever say it any other way. When everything else fell to pieces, one could still believe in the possibilities of America, out there on the other side of night, the other side of the world.

Al now drove his car on a thin wagon trail running alongside barbed-wire fences, both following the folds of the foothills. "What's the matter with this crowd?" Al finally said. "Can't you talk?"

"It's the Hills," Hayden said. "You just want to look."

Erik glanced back at him. Hayden had a strong face, bushy eyebrows, rugged features, and a short-cropped mustache. A good face for a portrait. . . .

At last Al drove up a long grade. At the top, a small lonely wooden church stood in the middle of a cemetery, just like the old country. Al braked in front of the gate, and then reconsidered and drove on past it. "So Ma won't have so far to walk."

They got out, and Al reached into the trunk of his car for a sickle.

"Looks like the church is dead too," Hayden said.

"Yeah." Al nodded. "It ain't been used for a helluva long time."

A spindly steeple perched on the west end like an afterthought, with only an empty cavity where the bell had hung, and a lightning rod on top.

They walked single file past the church. The windows were all boarded up.

"Used to go there purdy reg'lar. Ma made me." Al hooked his sickle between boards and tried to peek through a crack. "Can't see a damn thing."

Hayden exchanged looks with Louise. "Didn't do much good, did it?"

"What?" Al said.

"Going to church."

"Couldn't get int'rested, seems like. I guess it done some folks a lot o' good, all right. Kinda reminded 'em of the old country. They carried on some purdy fancy singin' in there."

Hayden nodded. "I expect."

"You darn right. Pa he used to blast away, by golly, you'd think he meant it." Al looked around to make sure they were all listening. "Just let 'em have it, you know–hung onto the last note till everybody else petered out."

Then he pointed with the sickle, like a crescent moon on a handle. "It's down that way, in the corner." They followed him through the weeds.

The grave had a plaque with her name and dates and a Bible verse in Danish. They stood for a moment looking in silence. Then Al kneeled and started to cut the dry grass and weeds.

"You're named after her, I expect," Hayden said to Louise.

She nodded.

"Yeah." Al peered up. "Darn purdy little sister. The folks sure missed her. They'd come up here in the evenings sometimes. Couldn't git over it, seems like."

"You'd better get busy," Louise said, "if you're going to finish before they come."

Al looked from her to Hayden. "That's a woman for you. Always so damn practical." Still kneeling, he whacked at the dry grass.

Erik had moved closer to Louise, and now he trailed her through the shaggy grass to read other names on the stones and markers.

Hayden followed. "Must be an old cemetery. I notice some dates go back to the gold strike in the Hills." He took out a notebook.

"Going to write it up for the paper?" Louise asked.

"Maybe. I've been working on a little article about the Hills."

"I expect Grandpa can tell you a lot about this place."

Hayden nodded, copying an inscription. "I don't suppose anybody brought a camera."

"No," Louise said. "We don't have one. You want to take pictures?"

"Just the church."

Louise suddenly turned to Erik. "You could draw it, couldn't you?"

Hayden looked at him too. "D'you draw?"

"Sure," Louise said. "He was a painter in the old country."

"That so? I didn't know that," Hayden said.

"I haven't done it for a long time," Erik objected.

"Please," Louise begged. She turned to Hayden. "You have anything to draw on?"

"Only my notebook, I'm afraid." He handed it and his pencil to Erik. "I'd be much obliged."

Erik hesitated. "The church?" He glanced up at it.

"This ought to make a good easel." Hayden put his hand on the sloping top of a tombstone. "Here, let me help hold the notebook for you."

"I don't know," Erik wavered. He looked at the church again. And then into Louise's eager blue eyes.

"You could maybe let it run over on the next page," Hayden suggested.

Hayden and Louise stood watching when Erik relented. And after a little while, Al came over with his sickle. "What's goin' on here, anyway? Oh, I see. Makin' a pitcher, ha? By golly, that ain't bad. Nossir. Not half bad. Not much to it, I guess, if you know how."

Erik said nothing, even though he was so tense he had to work at keeping his arm from shaking. And then they all glanced up at the sound of Chris's car, pulling up at the gate. Al waved. "Be right over," he shouted at the top of his lungs.

The road climbed diagonally up the steep rocky hillside above a gorge. From his side of the car, Erik could look almost straight down at the tops of pines and a miniature stream wriggling at the bottom far below.

Beside him, Al shifted the car to low with a ripping of gears. He turned briefly to Erik. "Hope we don't meet anybody." Al had pushed his hat back, and the stiff brim circled his face like a faded halo. A bead of sweat ran down his cheek.

The nearly vertical hillside was hot. Erik could feel Louise's fingers touching the back of his neck. He didn't dare look down anymore. The roadway cut into the side of the cliff on the left. Ahead it looked as if the road leaped off into space.

The car barely crawled along now and Al, hugging the vehicle close to the rock wall, abruptly turned in his seat to stare at the road behind them.

With Al distracted, his car began to stray away from the cliff wall, into the middle and then across the center of the road, toward the drop-off on Erik's side. Erik stiffened. In the next frozen seconds, Erik stared at the steering wheel, Al's brown hands on it, and then at his own hands–clutched, holding back, impotent.

"My God!" Hayden grabbed Al's seat.

Al quickly turned back around, and jerked the wheel towards the cliff face.

Erik remembered to breathe again, feeling like he'd just jolted awake from a nightmare, right before a terrible fall. Sunlight reflected brightly from the rocky curving cliff wall. Blue sky stretched over it all–the pure blue sky, spilling to the horizon and the hills below, and settling in the valleys.

The car drove smoothly again and Al shifted it into second, but Erik still braced himself stiffly.

"Thought I heard Chris's car," Al finally explained.

No one answered.

Erik sighed loudly as he slid one tense foot loose on the slanting floorboard, and then the other. He noticed his shoes were dusty from the dry grass in the churchyard. Pale-faced, he bent to brush off his cuffs. Up until the last frightful moment, he had sat there without moving, without reaching for the wheel to save them all.

"Damn fool stunt for me to pull, on this kind of a road," Al admitted.

"A-men." Hayden settled back in his seat again.

Al was about to turn his head again but caught himself. He wouldn't be distracted twice, Erik thought. Erik would take over the wheel next time. But a next time wouldn't happen. The time for action had passed, and he'd missed it.

Al drove away from the gorge now, still high up but out in the open. Erik recognized this as the part of the Hills where the dark cloud had risen the night he'd met Louise on the trail. The night they'd ridden home together over the divide. Then he'd had her to himself, as they watched the full moon riding into the Dakota sky.

He hadn't dared take over the wheel. Was she thinking that too?

They rode up and down, the road like a ribbon around the flared skirt of the Hills.

It hadn't been up to him. To do anything. He was just along. As usual.

Two hills lay ahead. Erik had seen them many times from the divide, from the gate, and when coming home in the evening. They stood a little apart, by themselves, as if left alone.

Before reaching them, Al turned off the road, onto a trail into a draw. The sides closed in and became wooded. Over the treetops domed the Hills, dark green mounds with morning haze misting through the deep recesses between them. The trail was rutted, where the spring thaws had run, Al explained. And then suddenly an opening appeared, a wide canyon, with a stream coming down, splashing and glinting down over its rocky bed. The trail turned up the left bank, and wound with the stream along the foot of the canyon wall, brick red at first, changing to brown as Al drove on, and then to slate and back to brown, on both sides. Sunlight slanted through the pines along the rim to the canyon floor.

"See the turrets up there," Louise exclaimed.

"Like something out of a story book, isn't it?" Hayden said.

"And there's the path you have to climb to rescue the princess." Louise pointed.

Erik watched the rocky towers until the canyon wall cut them off.

"Quite a few raspberries along here," Al added.

"Any chokecherries?–I hope not," Louise said. "Or we'll spend the afternoon picking."

"Not me," Al said firmly.

"No?" Louise asked.

"No, by golly."

"Mamma packed the pails."

"Don't give a damn if she did."

"We'll strike," Louise said. "I hope."

"You and me both, kid. You darn right."

They passed a side canyon to the left, and through its opening they could see a naked rust-colored hill rising above pine-covered slopes. It was only visible for a moment, and then the limestone canyon wall reappeared and plummeted into a belt of aspen, and presently they came to a log bridge across a brook. Without slowing, Al cramped the car, and it bounced over the bridge and into an open space among the pines.

"Well, folks, this is it." Al shut off the engine and then cocked his head to listen. The muted sounds of a waterfall resonated from the canyon wall. "I remember that sonofagun." Al got out, followed by the others, Louise brushing down her skirt behind.

"It's funny," Al said. "You ever had the experience like something happened before? By golly, for a minute I felt like this had happened exactly the same way once before."

"Well, you've been here before, haven't you?" Hayden said.

"Yeah, but that ain't what I mean. It's more like I dreamed it."

"Maybe you did." Louise tried to brush her pale, windblown hair back into place with her fingers.

"Well, it don't make no difference, I guess." Al shrugged.

"Things get stuck in memory," Hayden remarked, "even when you don't notice. Mostly when you don't notice."

"Yeah," Al drawled. "I don't know. It's easy to remember this place. It don't change much. Just about like it was when I was a kid. Used to come up here after logs with Pa and Chris. It's like something standing still. Even the waterfall. It's been going like that ever since."

They listened to the pouring sound.

"Yeah," Al said. "Things change a little out there." He made a gesture back in the direction they had come from. "I was thinking when we was in the cemetery, seeing that old church and all, how much has happened since we first came to this country. You don't think about it so much when you're out there."

"No," Hayden said. "It helps to get away from it. You get up on a hill here, and the whole country out there is just a gray streak on the horizon."

"Oh, I don't know," Al protested. "I wouldn't say that."

A windshield flashed from the trail, and they watched Chris's car crawl slowly and ease across the bridge to them.

"Well, I see you made it all right," Julia said, after they pulled up.

"Darn right." Al went to help his mother. "Your foot any better since you started using that horse liniment?"

"How you talk," Martha said wearily, putting her arm on his shoulder. "The doctor is doing the best he knows."

"Sure." He handed over her crutch. "Sure he is. But, by golly, that ain't enough. If you don't start gettin' better purdy quick, I'm gonna take you along to Omaha when I ship the steers. You darn right."

Martha's hair was turning white, the transparent white of aging blond hair. It was thin, parted in the middle, and drawn to a knot at the back. Yes, Louise took after her. Erik had noticed it before.

Julia began to unload the car.

"Gonna eat right away?" Al asked.

"Well, we're going to get ready." Julia handed him a cardboard box. "You better get the fire built." She nodded at a blackened stone fireplace.

"You bet."

She turned to Erik. "You want to fetch a pail of water? There's a spring up the trail a little ways."

"I'll show him," Louise volunteered.

"No, you stay here and help me," Julia said. "I'm sure Erik can find it by himself."

Erik took the new pail, and Louise handed him the dipper. Julia watched both of them while Erik walked away. He gazed back longingly as he turned off the bridge. Why hadn't Julia wanted Louise to come with him? Louise stood watching Al collect wood for the fireplace. How graceful she looked from the back, her feet together.

A thorny twig brushed Erik. It drooped with raspberry clusters, plump and juicy. He stopped to taste them, puckering his tongue. The sweetness and wildness! Below him the brook chuckled quietly over its stones. And beyond the brook lay the stillness of the canyon, a deep, nearly impenetrable hush. Behind him, the gentle sound of the waterfall dropped down the side of silence, revealing the width of the canyon.

Erik turned to gaze at the thin transparent veil, hanging over the canyon wall, as if suspended there. Sunlight caught in the spray, and he could hear the waterfall cascading down behind a row of aspen, standing like a choir of tall girls in front.

Erik hurried on. Back on the farm it was time for Gus to water the horses and feed the pigs. How many lonely Sundays he had gone out to do it and stared up at the Black Hills, and up the section lane toward the knolls, hoping the family would return soon, with Louise.

As Erik walked back carefully with the full pail, he saw smoke rising in the pines and heard indistinct voices. Louise leaned over the railing of the bridge, waiting for him. She wanted a drink, and he drew the dipper up full to the brim. Too cold for her to finish, she was about to throw away what was left.

"I'll take it," he stopped her. Thinking she would have instinctively taken the wheel.

After he drank, she helped carry the pail. "Better than going to church, isn't it? But I guess you wouldn't know," she added mischievously.

He smiled back. "Unless this is it."

"This?" She looked around. "Yes. I hadn't thought of it in that way. I've never seen a big church."

He paused momentarily to shift his hand on the handle. He had gone to a cathedral back home. The little wooden structures here seemed so out of place for such a big land. Was that what Hayden had thought too, why he had wanted the sketch?

Water slopped over the edge of the pail, and they stopped again.

Al shook the big coffee pot they used for threshers, rattling the lid. "A little service here!" he called, while Julia looked up and frowned.

Mayland stood up from the picnic blanket spread on the ground. "Anybody want to go along up the canyon a ways?"

"Sure." Hayden stood up. He glanced doubtfully at Julia. "Maybe the ladies would like some help with the dishes first."

"No, that's all right," Julia said. "You go on ahead."

Al gulped his coffee. "Wait a minute."

"Ain't you going?" Mayland asked Chris.

"Naw, I guess not."

"He has to have his nap first," Julia added.

Erik was sitting by Louise. "Don't you want to go?" she asked.

He shook his head. "I'll help clean up."

They watched Mayland, Al, and Hayden cross the bridge, and then just their heads were visible, moving above the bushes along the brook.

"I s'pose they'll go on up to see that old miner," Julia said.

Chris didn't reply. He was stretching out along the edge of the blanket.

"Always the darn dishes," Louise complained.

"Watch your language, Louise," her mother warned. "That's no way for a young lady to talk. Is it, Grandma?"

"Young lady, phooey. That's all I hear. This is a picnic, isn't it?"

Erik glanced sympathetically at Louise, but she didn't return his look.

Julia didn't say anything more, and then only the clicking of dishes filled the silence.

Chris was asleep on the blanket when they finished.

"I wonder if he's going to sleep all afternoon." Julia removed her apron and stood undecided. "I wanted to pick some chokecherries."

"We can do it," Erik quickly volunteered, thinking of Louise, and remembering too late what she had said about it in Al's car.

"Well. If you want to." Julia still looked uncertain, but then she turned to Louise. "You better stay with Grandma till Papa wakes up."

Louise nodded.

Erik tried not to look back at her. Now he had only a chore to get through now, and it was already getting late.

"I saw some nice ones from the car." Julia led the way. She took such short steps, and the canyon wall glowed hot from the sun. Erik felt like he was going back to work. "Chris said maybe you'd rent Gus's place when he leaves."

"I don't know."

For a while the only sounds came from their shoes scuffling on the trail and the pails jiggling on their handles.

"Well, there's no hurry, I guess," Julia said at last.

Erik still hoped Louise might come help when her father woke up. Maybe she'd just get tired of sitting there.

"I see you can draw, all right," Julia tried again. "I thought that was pretty good of the church. Only I don't care so much for that kind. Too rundown to suit me."

Erik only nodded.

"I used to paint some," Julia added.

He nodded again.

"I got two in the parlor. You must have seen them."

"I remember."

"There's another in the bedroom, one I made for a church bazaar. Chris kind of liked it and bought it back. It's of Harney Peak. About that big." She indicated the size of the painting with her hands. "Harney Peak is up in the Hills a ways, the highest point. I'd like to go there sometime."

Perplexed, he looked at her, wondering if he had misunderstood.

"I copied it from a postcard," Julia explained. "Looks just like it. That's what they say." She had stopped, and stared across the brook. "Quite a few trees along there. I wonder if we can get across."

He helped her down the bank and pushed ahead through the bushes, holding branches back for her. The water was shallow, and they soon found stepping stones across it. The trees were full. Nobody had gotten there ahead of them. They picked cherries they could reach from the ground, pulling limbs down, and occasionally broke them. Erik thought it felt like a kind of rough vandalism. But he too was in a hurry to fill his pails, and they both rushed impatiently from one unfinished tree to the next.

Louise still didn't appear, and after a while Erik gave up on her. Julia guessed that Chris would follow the other men. There was no telling, she said, how long they'd be gone if they stopped to visit with the old miner. They would have to review his rock collection.

And the picking continued until their pails were full.

"Well," Julia said at last, "that wasn't so bad."

"No," Erik lied.

"We don't come up to the Hills every day. It's nice to have something to show for it." She took such tiny steps that Erik had to hold himself back.

Chris was sitting on the blanket talking with his mother when they finally returned.

"They haven't come back yet?" Julia said.

"Naw. Not yet." Chris reached out to sample the cherries.

"I don't know why they'd be gone so long," Martha said.

Julia untied her sunbonnet. "Where's Louise?"

"Ain't she comin'?" Chris asked.

"Coming?" Julia gave him a puzzled look.

"I thought she was with you."

Julia shook her head.

Chris spit out his cherry seeds. "That's funny."

Julia stood watching him, and he got up.

"How long since Louise left?" she demanded.

Chris fidgeted. "An hour, I s'pose." He glanced back at his mother. "An hour and a half, maybe."

"And you didn't see which way she went?"

"Probably pickin' cherries some place," Chris ventured.

"I'll go and look," Erik said quickly, but they acted as if they hadn't heard him.

"You say you didn't see her down your way a'tall?" Chris returned to his first thought.

"I told you," Julia snapped.

"No need to git sore." Chris's gaze followed Julia's up the trail, and he quickly took up the suggestion. "Maybe she left to meet the others."

Julia turned to Martha. "You didn't see her?"

"No, Julia. I didn't. It's a wonder Louise didn't say something."

"Oh, that's the way she is." Chris shook his head. "Anyway, they oughta return purdy quick."

"And if she didn't go up that way?" Julia persisted.

"Well, there's only one other place, and that's up the side canyon. I s'pose it wouldn't hurt to take a turn over that way." Chris abruptly called Louise's name, and then again, louder. His echo rebounded from the canyon wall, unanswered. Chris realized he would have to go look, and he turned to Erik. "You wanta come along?"

Julia followed them to the bridge.

"We'll be back purdy quick." Chris struck out.

Erik found it difficult to keep up with him. Very different from walking with Julia. Erik couldn't remember ever seeing Chris and Julia walking together–even to the car. Chris called again, and not even an echo answered this time. "The darnedest kid to run off like that."

Except at its entrance, the side canyon had no walls, only long pine-covered slopes, and the rusty wedge of a bare hill turning red. Chris and Erik kept near the middle of the side canyon, and studied both sides as they strode up it.

"Well, I think this is a wild goose chase," Chris said after a while. He glanced at the sun. "Gittin' late, too." He called again, and they listened. "Naw," he said more softly, "I expect she went to meet the men. Julie gits kinda excited."

He paused a moment when they returned to the trail. "You're sure she didn't come down this way?"

"I think she would have seen us." Erik showed him where they'd picked chokecherries.

"Yeah, you'd think so." Chris led the way back to their picnic area. Mayland, Al, and Hayden had returned, but Louise wasn't with them.

"I have a hunch you didn't go far enough, Chris," Al said.

Hayden checked his watch. "I wonder if somebody shouldn't drive up to the government station before it gets too late."

Julia put her handkerchief to her eyes, and Hayden went over to her. "Probably just went farther than she thought," he tried to comfort her.

"Yeah, it fools you all right," Al chimed in. He turned to Chris. "You go on up to the ranger station and I'll walk back down where you was. Take another look anyway. Maybe Hayden will go along if he can stand it."

"Sure," Hayden said.

"You stay here then, Pa," Al ordered, "and holler like the devil if she comes. Not you women now, so we can tell if Louise calls out."

For a moment Erik was afraid they'd leave him out. Maybe Chris would let him ride along up to the ranger station. But as Erik moved toward the car, Al turned to him. "You better go down the trail a ways. Just to make sure."

Erik nodded. Al probably knew it was useless but maybe he wanted to give Erik something to do.

Julia pulled the blanket out of the way the car, and quickly turned her face. Al saw it. "Gosh." He put his arm around her shoulder. "Don't you worry now. We ain't far into the Hills, you know. If we don't find her purdy quick, we'll git the troops from Fort Meade. You darn right." His voice quivered.

Al and Hayden turned into the side canyon, and Erik continued on down the main trail. The shadow from the opposite canyon wall already streaked the path in places. He passed the spot where he and Julia had crossed the brook. He had glanced up many times while they were picking. He would have seen Louise passing by. And if she didn't want to help pick, she would have avoided them by not coming this way at all. This was clearly useless.

"Louise," he called anyway. Then louder. Echoes bounced back from the other side. How strange he felt, shouting her name. Always before he had only whispered it. An eagle wheeled above the canyon wall ahead, and then soared on over an upward thrust of rock, which looked like a tower with pines at its base. Like the rocky turrets Louise had exclaimed over.

The turrets!

Erik stopped, memories crowding in as if to smother him.

He started walking fast, then ran. She had always spent time alone too, played alone, ridden alone. She wasn't afraid–walking across the creek flume, or climbing Broken Rock when she was a little girl.

He ran out of breath and reluctantly slowed back down to a walk. The near wall receded from the trail, beginning with a steep incline at the foot of it. The shadow from the far wall began to creep up the incline. How still it felt with evening coming on!

If only Louise would appear out of the shadows. A sharp turn appeared to the right ahead. Perhaps even now she approached from the other side. He slowed near the bend to delay peering around it. Or maybe she had started up the path and couldn't go on. She might have fallen and hurt herself–just a little, maybe twisted an ankle–so he would have to carry her back.

Even before the trail led him around the turn, he glimpsed the rock turrets above the canyon rim, bright and shimmering. But on foot he found no fairy tale path to them, only a dislodged portion of the canyon wall which had cut a swath part way down. Around the bend the real trail remained as empty as before. Erik turned off and scrambled diagonally up the slope. He could always turn back.

It seemed like any other steep hillside at first, with bush branches to hold onto and an occasional pine. He could certainly get up to the deposits from the cave-in, and on over them to the foot of the wall. She couldn't have climbed that. Surely not.

He sat down to rest when he emerged from the bushes. From here on only imbedded rocks would give him footing until he reached the fallen slabs. And when he started up again he realized he would have to crawl. After a little he couldn't even do that. He had to lean down flat, brace his shoes against the rocks, and clutch at those above him. He accidentally dislodged a stone, and heard it bounce behind him and crash through the bushes below.

He lay still for a minute, then propped himself up on his elbow. He could see a young pine only a yard above him. He ended up propelling himself up to it like a snake, breathing the hot dust. He wiped his face on his shirt sleeve and reached out fiercely, crushing pine needles around the trunk in his hand.

He lay there, breathing hard. She couldn't have done this. It was useless going on. But he would only need to move his own length now. This was the same feeling he got when he painted–it wouldn't let him stop, as if his muscles made him go on. He began to inch himself past the pine, digging the sides of his shoes in until he wedged one against the slim trunk, and then he clawed at the edge of the lowest rock slab.

In a moment he was on it and then up on the next. How still it was, and hot! He peered back over his shoulder toward the opposite canyon rim, and then quickly up ahead again. A lone bird flew past the turrets. He held his breath listening, but again he sensed mostly only a hushed silence. A tremor shivered slowly down his spine. Had he heard a cry?

He stood at last, and made his way up over the heap of jagged stone fragments along the canyon wall. He found some natural steps up, only several centimeters wide. He tried the first and then the second. But the next was higher. He lifted his foot slowly, feeling for the step, and then straightened his leg like a lever. Then he stood shaking, the palms of his hands flat against the wall, on dry sunburnt rock.

He would have to slip sideways now to a protruding ledge. He began to slide his feet along the edge. He had to go up a little, but he found a fracture in the wall to hold on to. Then he suddenly discovered the fissure was wide enough so he could pull himself up into it and climb it like the inside of a chimney.

The fissure did not lead all the way to the top, but it opened into a cavity from which most of the rockfall had dropped. He found barely enough room to stand. He glanced down and then instantly to the front, and grasped a sticky root hanging down. As he hung there and looked up and back, Erik could barely see the tip of a tall pine above the rim, its top touching the sky.

He released the root and dropped to his knees. He would have to go back—if he could. He turned his head slowly to look down. What would they think if they spotted him up here? He shivered as he remembered the narrow steps on the wall below.

He couldn't do that again, not going down. His knees hurt, and he braced his hands against the wall. Finally he stood up and reached for the root again. It seemed like barely more than a stub, as big around as his wrist. The wall was concave, with a projection on it half way up–enough to put his feet on if he could get up to it.

He grasped the root with both hands and climbed it, hand over hand, bracing his feet against the wall, one past the other, until he reached the top rim of the cavity. He could put most of his weight on it, and he reached over the rim. He felt a rough protrusion, a surface root. He tested it, pulling on it as hard as he could. Then he also let go of the hanging root with his other hand, clamped down on the cavity edge and heaved himself up over.

It took him only a moment to lay flat on his face, with his arms around the base of the sunlit tree trunk.

He dragged himself away from the rim, his heart still pounding. Sunlight beamed horizontally on pine trunks and lit up a brown carpet of needles. The bark of a Norway pine standing by itself gleamed as if inlaid with Black Hills gold.

Erik pushed on his elbow and sat up, facing the sun and the canyon. He couldn't climb down again. What if they had already found Louise and were ready to start for home, and expected to meet him on the trail or overtake him? They wouldn't think of looking up. Even if he shouted, they wouldn't hear him up here.

He frantically scrambled to his feet. He turned again towards the rock towers, very near now, behind a fringe of pines. He started towards them, on nearly level ground covered with dead needles. A big pine lay across his path, and he changed directions to get around it. Near the tree's top he started to step across it, pushing its branches aside. Suddenly he fell back from a steep drop-off.

Directly across the chasm rose a towering cliff, splitting into the turrets on top. Now he wouldn't have so far to go to reach the final base of the turrets, but first it was straight down. He couldn't go this way.

Erik stepped back around the fallen trunk to follow the flat, needle-coated ledge high above the trail. That was all he could do now; search for another way to climb down, or continue along this way, if necessary, as far as the entrance to the side canyon. He tried to remember if there was a slope. Al and Hayden would pass directly below on their way back. It wouldn't matter what they said or thought. If the fire was still going he would be able to spot that, and maybe they could hear him from there.

He soon realized the upper slopes of the side canyon stretched out before him, purpling swells with the evening haze on them as far as he could see. He felt like he was soaring above them. Probably no one had ever walked up here before.

What had drawn him here? Once the hunch came over him, Erik had continued to climb as if he had to. He might rationalize it for himself but not for others. Anyone would know Louise couldn't have done this. Had he really known it from the beginning, and later had he not heard a human cry, but only the shriek of a bird? Yet from the time he had started up from the canyon trail, he'd had no other choice.

He had wanted to; he had needed to do this. To not turn back. To not flee.

He saw another tower-like thrust he had noticed from below. The pines thinned out at its base, exposing the limestone, moss-grown like an ancient graveyard. And over the ledge, far out, a bald mountain rose suddenly like a giant red moon. From below it hadn't looked this big.

Erik realized he'd come to a stop, and then all at once he spotted a ravine-like cleft crossing the ledge. Instinctively he followed it on the chance it might lead to a way down. It dropped him from level to level off to the left, and then widened toward an opening. When he emerged he stood level with the tops of trees below. In the next instant he saw that the shelf-like mountain stairway descended all the way down into the side canyon. A frightened brown squirrel leaped ahead of him.

The slope below was wooded, and he found a small brook at the bottom. He knelt down at the edge to drink, in the evening shade and coolness. He raised his head before drinking again. He would remember this tiny stream here in the folds of the mountains, spilling over stones like a chain of miniature waterfalls. Then he heard a rustling among bushes on the other side, and another shiver ran down his spine.

"Lou-ise." His voice went up.

She stopped. "Oh, there you are."

He stood up.

She walked on up to the stream bank. "You didn't see me, did you? I waved."

He couldn't answer.

"I spotted you way up there–what's the matter?"

He wiped his face.

"How you look." She started across, stepping on stones, and he held out his hand to her.

"Oh, Louise." He tried to keep his voice steady. "You know they're all out searching for you."

"You're kidding." She took his hand. "It isn't that late. Is it?"

"Didn't you know?"

"Who's searching?"

He couldn't answer for a moment. How soft and warm her hand felt in his.

"Uncle Al?" she said.

He nodded. "And Mr. Hayden."

"Not Papa?"

"He drove up to the government station."

"What for?–No!"

"Yes."

She took her hand back. "We'd better hurry."

They struck out single file at first. How agile she was, reminding Erik of the time she had danced ahead of him on the flume.

"I didn't want to pick chokecherries," Louise said, when they escaped the thicket and could walk side by side. "We always have to do that." She glanced at him. "Which way did Uncle Al and Hayden go?"

He told her.

After a little she said, "I guess I've spoiled it for everybody. Papa will sure be mad, won't he?"

He only shook his head.

"No?" She was silent for a moment. "I see."

They strode out into the open and peered back up into the side canyon.

"You remember the turrets we saw from the car?" she said.

He could only nod.

"You can see them from this side too." She glanced back. They both turned around for a moment to admire the towers. "I didn't notice them right away," she said as they moved on. "But it's farther than you think. I got into some places you can hardly get through." She wasn't looking at him but down the slope. "Isn't that Uncle Al and Hayden?" She began to holler and wave.

They saw her, Al swinging his hat back and forth over his head.

Then they all ran.

"Hi," Al shouted as they came within earshot. "You all right?"

"Sure."

Al wiped his forehead, his hat tilted back. "Holy gee-whiz!"

Louise smiled at him impishly.

"Come here, let me look at you," Al said.

She stuck her tongue out.

Al reached out for her and clasped her waist. "Don't you ever do that again. You hear? Or I'll spank the livin' daylights out o' you."

Louise laughed.

"By golly, you sure had us scared. No foolin'."

"Al was about to send the troops out," Hayden said.

"Damn right! Where the devil did you go?"

Louise gave Al a defiant look.

"Well?" Al persisted.

"We decided not to pick chokecherries," she said. "Remember? You got out of it, didn't you?"

Al glanced at Hayden. "What's so funny?"

Smiling, Hayden shook his head. "I didn't say anything."

"I didn't say you did, but, by golly, you was thinking it." Al started to laugh and then noticed Erik. "For God's sake! Look at you! Where the hell have you been?"

"Oh," Erik started.

Louise came to his rescue. "He looked for me way up the hillside."

"By gosh, you look like you've been in a fight." Al stared at him.

Erik tried to smile.

"Up the hillside, huh?" Al repeated. "And that's how you found her?"

"No," Louise said. "I found him."

Al laughed. "That's a good one." He started to laugh again and suddenly stopped. "How come you was up there? I thought you went down the trail. You was headin' that way when we last seen you." He turned to Hayden and then back to Erik. "How did you get over here? That's what I'd like to know."

"Oh," Erik started again.

But Louise's wide eyes were also on him now. "No! You didn't climb up the canyon wall! Did you?"

"You goddamn fool," Al blurted out. "Jesus Christ almighty–"

Louise wheeled on her uncle with a flinty stare like her father's. "Shut up, you."

Al looked as if he'd been struck.

Louise's lips trembled, and she quickly put her hand to her eyes. "Erik came all that way for me–don't you dare yell at him."

"Here." Hayden moved over to her and pulled a rumpled red handkerchief out of his pocket. She blew her nose in it. "Al didn't mean it," Hayden pleaded.

"'Course not," Al said hurriedly.

Louise gazed back at him with misty eyes.

"I'm sorry," Al said, and Louise finished wiping her eyes.

"Suppose we go on ahead," Hayden suggested to Al, "and let the folks know."

"Sure. You bet." Al turned once more to Erik. "By golly, I don't see how you done it."

Hayden was waiting for Al.

"You kids better wash off a little in the crick first," Al added. "But don't take too long."

Erik watched the two men walk out of sight around a cluster of pines. Louise still had her back to him.

"Al didn't mean it," Erik repeated.

Louise turned toward him. "How awful," she said. Then she suddenly rose on her toes and put her bare arms around his neck.

"Lou–" The rest smothered on her lips, soft, warm, and pressing.

He felt a tug on the back of his neck even after it ended. She still had her hand on his shoulder.

"How pretty!" she said.

Together they gazed back towards the turrets, rising out of the pines, standing high, shimmering, and crowned by sunlight. Erik glowed with tired happiness, which would help him find his way back, at last alone again with Louise. Alone with Louise! He had won the princess.

6

Autumn arrived, and Erik forgot about the sudden downpours of spring. Intermittent sheets of driving rain now soaked through his overalls and shoes, cold and wet. He drove Louise to school in the buggy and returned for her in the afternoons. Until the rainy weather set in, the buggy had stood abandoned in a back corner of the machine shed. Then Louise remembered it. Chris had gotten into the habit of simply taking the lumber wagon, always parked handy by the end of the barn, whenever the roads turned bad.

The weather blotted out the Black Hills, and the country suddenly seemed smaller. Sitting half-enclosed with Louise under the black buggy top and slanting rain, Erik became only conscious of time slowing and a lulling sense of contentment. This was what his long summer had finally brought him.

"It's nice, isn't it?" Louise said. "The buggy, I mean."

Erik looked at her hopefully.

"Sometimes Papa says he's going to sell it, but I don't think he will. He's had it so long. He bought it when he first started going with Mamma."

Erik nodded.

"'Course," she added, "Papa's not sentimental like Uncle Al."

Erik only nodded again, not daring to say anything lest he spoil it. This was the way it would begin for him, at first, his feelings spilling over just a little.

She looked across the meadows. Where they had sat together in the hot noon, during hay season. Where they had crossed on the flume. They couldn't see the empty homestead today. Rain and mist blurred the view all along the creek.

"A few days like this, and I'm good and ready for it to clear up again." Louise glanced at Erik. "Aren't you?"

"Oh." He hesitated. "I don't mind."

"You don't? Was Denmark like this a lot?"

"Ye-es."

"I don't know what you see in it."

"You."

He didn't look beyond Sally during the pause. He only listened. The rain had stopped. Sally's hooves slushed in tracks in the gumbo. Hadn't Louise heard him? Hadn't he said it loudly enough? Hadn't he said it? Finally he faced Louise.

She was gazing ahead, straight ahead, sitting there encased in her slicker, hood up over her head.

"I couldn't stand it," Louise said at last, "to live in a country where it's like this most of the time."

He looked down, noticing his soaked shoes, and the barnyard splotches on the cuffs of his overalls.

"Sally's dragging the singletree on the wheel," she added.

He busied himself with Sally. There was no getting back to where he'd been with Louise. Not this time. He would have to wait.

After dropping her off at school and turning back towards home alone, he sank into his old lonely feelings. He didn't try to make Sally pull up. He passed empty coal cars and bumped across the shallow irrigation ditch. The rain started up again. Paint peeled off a sign by the crossing. Look Out For Trains. Look Out. . . . The track ran straight across the flats, rails glistening and stunted rosin weeds growing between them. Once in a while a crew would ride out on a handcar and hoe them.

The buggy jolted across the rails and the cattle guard. "I couldn't stand it," he repeated to himself. That was what she had said. And when the weather cleared, he couldn't drive her anymore. He would return to the field again, and watch for her to ride by on Brownie in the morning, and follow her with his eyes as long as he could. And then he'd wait all afternoon, glancing toward the knolls and trying to be near the fence when she passed by again, if Chris wasn't there.

Erik looked toward Gus's. He couldn't spot his sod house today. Only the flat fields and the basin with wet smears of alkali, and puddles by the road. Erik stopped at the end of the barn and unhitched with cold fingers. Sally was fast enough getting through the door and into her stall. Erik still had a long wait until noon. He walked slowly across to the tool shed, to oil leather harness straps with neat's-foot oil which was all he had to do until it was time to return for Louise.

He studied the harness he had started on, and identified the rump strap. He heard the kitchen screen door thud, and he picked up an oily rag.

He glanced around when the shed door opened.

"Well, how's it going?" Chris asked.

"Fine."

Chris peered at the pile of harnesses in the corner. "Got enough oil, you think?"

Erik shook the can and held it out.

"Aha." Chris tried to look in the can. "I thought if you was gonna run out, you better git some more uptown." He turned to go. "Nice rain, all right."

"Yes," Erik agreed. Rain made the last sound he listened for at night and the first when he woke up.

He watched Chris through the window. Erik felt relief to see him go. Whenever Chris appeared there was always the chance he was coming to say he would go pick up Louise himself.

Chris didn't know how much the evening ride home with Louise meant to Erik. Even their morning ride was only preparation–like a prelude, followed by a deeper slower movement. As the day wore on, anticipation poured into Erik, filling him with unreasoning longing and ache: to be driving Louise home, just to be going home with her on the lonely road toward the darkening divide.

As usual, Erik arrived at Louise's school early, and waited for her, his eyes on the crowded doorway. He always felt a little quiver when he spotted her. Then he stepped down with a robe to help her into the buggy. He tucked the robe under her.

"You got the mail, I see." Louise picked it up from the seat.

He walked around the buggy, got up beside her, and drew the robe up over their laps.

She checked through the mail. He knew none of it was for her.

"Shucks." She stuffed the letters down between them, keeping only the newspaper. She flopped it open on her lap.

He drove slowly past empty coal cars. A thin green light shone from the block signal.

"Look here," she cried suddenly.

He looked down, and she held the paper in front of him, their heads close together. He noticed that more than the paper.

"I knew about it," she said. "But Mr. Hayden didn't want me to tell."

Then Erik saw it–his sketch of the church.

"He wanted to surprise you. Did you know about it? You did, didn't you?"

He shook his head.

"Aren't you pleased?"

Erik couldn't answer.

"Aren't you?" she insisted. "It certainly came out nice, for just a newspaper." She found the beginning of the article and began to read.

He could see the title: "'Along the . . .'" he read aloud and then stopped.

"'Margins,'" she assisted him. "'Along the Margins.'"

"Oh?"

"You know what margins are, I guess. The edges kind of borders, you know."

He nodded.

"I s'pose that's what this is all around here." She waved. "I s'pose that's what he means."

She started reading again but soon gave it up. "The buggy rocks so much." She studied his drawing again. "It's nice. Mr. Hayden thinks so too. He says you have a lot of talent."

Again Erik didn't reply, and Louise gazed at him. "Mr. Hayden thinks you're wasting your time. Working on a farm."

"Yes?"

"But you don't," she pried.

He had no answer.

"Well," she persisted, "all I can say is if I could draw like that. . . ."

"It isn't that."

She only looked at him.

"I can't," he said.

"Well, I s'pose you know best. O' course, it's none o' my business."

Erik fell silent again for a while. If he couldn't tell Louise, who could he tell? "I did want to once," he said at last, softly, letting it slowly spill out. Already it felt like such a long time ago, but it still pained him. "Becoming an artist was all I thought of."

Louise didn't say anything, but she wasn't reading.

"My father," he continued, "he wanted me to help on our farm. I was supposed to have it when I grew up."

She nodded.

"That was before he married again. He couldn't see it, why I'd waste time painting."

"You didn't have any brothers or sisters either," she said.

"No. Not then." He paused, unwanted memories returning. "I knew a painter. He was older, and took me along sometimes when he went sketching–on Sundays. His name was Brandt. He always had some of his drawings or paintings accepted by exhibits, and I never did. I asked him what was the matter with mine, and he said I was just copying. That I hadn't done anything original."

Erik paused again. They had reached the top of the knolls. They could barely see the house on the creek. Ragged clouds dragged low over the divide.

"And that's why you gave it up?" Louise finally asked.

Erik nodded. "That's when I began to think about coming to America."

"I see."

"I couldn't even stand to look at any of my old drawings or canvases."

"You didn't throw 'em away?" she asked breathlessly.

"No. My folks wanted to keep them. But my work wasn't any good. Just like anybody's–a winding road, maybe, with an old stone cottage, a church, a farm, or some other scene like that–the kind of pictures you see on calendars."

"What's wrong with that?" she asked.

"None of it was true. None of it was anything people didn't know already."

"It could still be true, couldn't it?"

"No." He shook his head, and struggled to explain. "It wasn't my truth. I wasn't putting any of my true feeling into my work. So it couldn't be a new truth for anyone else either. It's easy to make a farm in a picture, if you don't care about it. But if you have to live there, that's different. That was the trouble."

She looked at his illustration again. "D'you have to like the things you paint?"

"Well. . . " he hesitated. "In a way, you have to. You have to feel them. And to do that you have to know them. Really know them–from living with them. That's what I didn't do. Somehow I'd known it all along, but it was Brandt who actually told me. I'm glad he did. I started to paint too soon, you might say, before I knew anything about life."

"Well, maybe you'll go back to it then after a while."

"No. I don't care for it anymore."

"You mean," she said, "you like this better, just working on a farm?"

"Yes." He looked at her. "I guess so."

"Well, I was thinking maybe if you like it–this country–you'd get interested in painting again. You'd have something to paint then, wouldn't you?"

"Yes, but. . . ." He paused, trying once more to figure out how to say it. "It's better to live the kind of life you like. Isn't it? Than to paint it?"

"I don't know. Is it?"

"Sure."

"Well," Louise said, after a little while. "I wouldn't know, I guess. I've never wanted to be an artist."

Erik gazed across the wet cornfield and then the stubble, while his thoughts lingered on the many lonely days he spent watching the shadow creeping down the end of the barn. He spotted the draw where the horses had stopped after the runaway, and then he thought of Jes.

"He misspelled your name," Louise said.

"Oh?"

She folded the paper.

"You like this country?" Erik asked suddenly.

"Sure, I guess so. Why?"

"Oh, nothing," Erik said. "I was just wondering," as he thought about the empty homestead.

"I've never been any other place." Louise looked down.

"And you think you'll always stay here?"

"I s'pose," Louise said. "I've never thought about it. Why?"

"Well, you said this morning you didn't care so much for it in this kind of weather."

They had turned off on the trail and dipped into a gully. The buggy tilted toward Erik's side and Louise slid over against him. She laughed, and he could feel her breath on his face. He put his free arm around her. She didn't move. She didn't say anything. Disappointed, after a while he had to get out to open the gate, and she drove the horses through.

Frost came after the rain, and then Erik felt the glow of Indian summer, out in the fields and inside himself. Late one afternoon he drove to the lower meadow for a load of hay. From the stack he could see the flume, bright red timbers and galvanized trough, gleaming in the mellow light. He could conquer that too, and not have to crawl across on his knees after Louise. He felt his heart beating faster. He'd have time for it this evening. He could walk across–alone. Some deeds had to be done alone. He thought of the rattler he'd killed out on the prairie, and his perilous climb in the Hills.

After he finished loading the wagon with hay, he left his team tied to the fence enclosing the stack and headed along the bank of the ditch for the flume. No one was likely to see him, and he would return too soon to be missed. Finally he hesitated, breathing hard, having walked too fast. At last he climbed up on the flume. As usual no water ran in the ditch.

He reminded himself that the footbridge was put there to walk on. All he had to do was place one foot in front of the other and move straight ahead, without looking down. That was all there was to it.

The first plank wobbled a little. The sun had warped it. Someone really should nail down these boards. He would have to mention it to Chris. Somebody might lose his balance. Erik paused and glanced down. His left knee shook. He put his weight on it harder, but it wouldn't stop shaking. He could always climb down if he had to. Louise had walked across it easily and others had too. Why couldn't he keep from looking down? If he should just keep his eyes on the bridge, instead of letting them rove to the sides.

He really didn't have very far to go. He slid one foot past the other, riveting his eyes to each plank, and raising his arms horizontally. One, just one–one foot at a time–hardly more than a shuffle. She hadn't done it this way. It was wide enough to walk on–if he didn't stare directly down to check where to put his feet–if instead he looked a little ahead.

He had probably nearly reached the middle already. The other bank would soon rise under him. It would come up fast. He moved his left foot again now, to step it across a crack to the next plank. Then his right foot. He caught a glimpse of bushes on the other side already, and the branches of the big cottonwood. Now he could lengthen his stride. Nothing to it, once he made up his mind.

He stood for a moment looking back. What mattered was keeping his mind well out in front of where he was. Should he return the same way to reassure himself, or cross on the fallen tree this time? Get used to it gradually? He decided he felt satisfied with a start from one side tonight. By rights, that wobbly plank should be nailed down before another attempt anyway. And it was getting late anyway. He had a long drive home. He should return to the team or he'd miss supper.

He circled out around the wooded bank through the tall grass, tugging at the seeds. This could all be his, just for the asking. All this rich bottom land lay here waiting for somebody. The natural terrace against the divide, overlooking the Hills, did provide the ideal location for a shack. The sun was setting between the two dark hills, and he watched it sink ever so slowly into the purple haze.

Morning frosted the grass silver, and wood smoke rose straight up in the thin air. After breakfast Erik went out to husk corn. His wrists became sore at first. But as he moved down the days and the corn rows amidst the crushing sound of the wagon, the ripping of husks, and the yellow ears pounding against the side board, he knew he'd found something outside himself at last. He heard the train traveling down across the flats, but it stirred no longings in him now. It was only one of the sounds of Dakota. He could watch evening coming on without his old sense of loneliness. He'd see Louise at supper. They would sit together in the corner by the stove afterward, listening to her mother reading installments from the Ladies Home Journal.

Then one night after supper Gus knocked at the door.

Julia opened it. "Come in, Gus."

"T'anks." He came in, apologizing to her. "I vanted to talk vid Erik."

So the time had come for Erik to decide.

"Have a chair," Julia said.

"T'anks." Gus held his hat on his fat knees. "I vas vondering if you vant the place," he said to Erik.

Erik felt relieved when Julia spoke first. "So you're getting ready to go?"

"Two veeks now."

"Planning to be there in time for Christmas, I s'pose," Julia said.

"You-bet."

"Aha," Chris said. "How long you figger to be gone, Gus?"

"I git back next fall."

"And you're going to bring somebody back with you?" Julia said.

"I t'ank so."

"Well," Chris said, "it's up to the boy, I guess."

"He'd have to stay down there, I s'pose," Julia added.

"O' course," Chris answered. "Have to for the insurance anyhow."

"Oh, I see."

"I s'pose we could kinda run the two places together," Chris continued. "That is, as far as the work goes."

When Erik still had nothing to say, Gus swallowed uneasily. "Mat Burk vants it."

"Naw." Chris shook his head. "I wouldn't do that. Hell, you wouldn't know the place when you git back."

"No," Gus agreed. "Dat's vot I t'ank too." He turned to Erik. All three looked at him.

"Gives Erik a place to stay this winter anyway," Chris suggested. "I guess it's an easy house to keep warm, ain't it, Gus?"

"Sure t'ing. You-bet."

Louise closed a book on her lap, and silently took it with her into her room. Erik heard her door closing.

Erik had hardly listened to what everyone said. He just wondered why had Louise stood up and left without a word. Why had he never mentioned this to her? Was it another evasion on his part? He'd had lots of chances. He'd known this was coming. Maybe he was afraid she'd agree with everyone else. That she didn't care enough to defend him this time.

Chris, Gus, and Julia were waiting. They had already decided for Erik. His chair creaked. Gus turned his hat slowly on his knee. It just about fitted there. His sleeves were too short, showing his woolly wrists.

"Well," Erik began. It didn't sound like him, and he stopped to catch his breath. He couldn't meet their looks. He felt trapped, with nowhere to flee now. "All right," he heard himself say at last. His stomach sank.

Gus nodded. He was nearly bald on top, but all around his head his shaggy dark hair stuck out like a thatch over the short collar of his overall jacket.

"I expect you better go down there some day soon before Gus leaves," Chris said.

Erik nodded. "Ye-es."

"So he can show you around. Give you an idea of what there is to do, I s'pose." Chris glanced toward Gus.

"You-bet," said Gus.

"We'll be seeing you, won't we, before you go?" Julia added.

"You-bet." Gus nodded from one to the other and stood up.

Erik followed him out, and Chris closed the door behind them. They walked slowly toward the corral, in a silence broken only by the tread of their shoes on the hard gumbo.

"You t'ank it's gonna freeze tonight maybe?" Gus said at last.

Erik peered up at a sky full of stars, bright and cold. "I guess." He stood by while Gus untied his horse and then watched him ride out of sight. No use going back to the house now, but Erik walked back around it. No light shone from Louise's window. Then he retraced his steps and returned to the woodshed.

By this time next year it would all be over. November. . . . No, he didn't need to count it. December, January, February.

He'd arrived a year ago, come March. He told himself others had to live alone too–Al, Jes, and Fred out north. Some jobs had to be done alone. But Erik didn't fall asleep for a long time that night.

From the lower end of the cornfield, Erik spotted the train–an engine with two yellow coaches and a baggage car crossing the flats toward town. He knew Gus was waiting to get on it. By nightfall Gus would leave the Black Hills, after so many years. Erik saw the white streamer spilling from the engine and heard the lonely wail. Yes, lonely now. He felt empty inside. He drove the team into the next corn row, but the beat of the ears on the sideboard came slower and sometimes stopped altogether.

Erik ate supper in a stiff silence, but Louise finally smiled when Chris announced that Fred would come home with the cattle any day now. And then Al would take the steers to Omaha.

"Remember to give Erik his check," Julia piped up.

"Yeah, sure. Bring the checkbook, Louise. Might as well do it now." Chris turned to Erik. "If you got your things ready we can drive around to Gus's in the morning." He glanced at Julia. "I s'pose we'll be goin' to church."

"I was planning to."

Chris took the checkbook from Louise. "Got a pen?"

She went to get it.

"Ain't that your jacket down in the barn?" Chris asked next. "Hangin' by the window?"

"Yes, I guess so," Erik said.

"Better git it." Chris filled out the stub.

Erik's heart sank. Of course he'd need his jacket. Better git it, so he wouldn't have anything to come back for? He listened to the ticking of the clock and the scratching of Chris's pen. It was almost as if Erik had never been here at all, never counted for anything.

"Here you are. I guess that's right, ain't it?" Chris held out the check.

Erik nodded. "Thanks." He rose swiftly to go, afraid he might speak his feelings aloud.

"Still wet, I guess," Chris warned.

Erik held the check between his thumb and forefinger. "Goodnight."

"G'night."

"'Night," Louise said, and she quickly turned away before Erik could hug her.

Erik closed the door behind him and didn't let the screen door slam. His last night. He walked down to the barn, and searched for the jacket Mayland had bought for him his first day. He felt his way in the dark, and ran his fingers through a cobweb to the coat. It had hung there all fall. Outside he shook the dust off and emptied the pockets. He found only some grains of wheat, a wad of twine, and a few staples. He put the staples back so car tires wouldn't pick them up.

In the woodshed he lit a lantern and got out his suitcase. He dusted it off with his jacket, so he could read the steamship labels again. The bright lock snapped open under his sun-browned fingers, releasing a persistent smell of newness, and the memory of the day he'd packed to leave home. His suitcase would go with him wherever he went, stand there, wait for him, and remind him of where he'd been.

He sat on the bed a long time, and when he glanced out at it, the kitchen was dark. Only a dim lantern light shone out on the divide, while the earth turned relentlessly toward another morning. Tomorrow night he would spend alone in Gus's house.

When Erik returned from watering the horses the next morning, Chris followed him into the barn. "Julia thinks I better take you before going to town. We got the time anyway."

Erik nodded. "All right."

"Yeah," Chris said. "Might as well, I guess. Won't take long."

Might as well, Erik thought bitterly. Just a chore, to get out of the way. The sooner the better. They walked in silence to the house. Neither had anything more to say. They cleaned their shoes on the scraper. But Chris waited politely for Erik to finish, so they could enter the house together.

"Good morning," Julia chirped.

A cardboard box sat against the wall just inside the door.

Julia nodded towards it. "That's for you. Just a few things I thought you might need."

"Thanks," Erik said.

"I put in a couple sheets and a pillow case to use for a while. I don't s'pose Gus has any. Except what's on the bed."

"Naw." Chris chuckled. "I don't s'pose he's even got any on the bed, does he?"

"Sure he does," Julia countered quickly. "Louise! Breakfast!"

The men washed and sat down at the table. Julia brought platters of pancakes and bacon from the stove and poured coffee. She passed a cup to Erik. "Oh, I meant to tell you to leave your laundry."

"That's all right." Erik had already stuffed it in a cardboard box with other belongings he couldn't fit in his suitcase.

"Just leave it on your bed," Julia continued. "I'll put it in the wash tomorrow."

Erik heard Louise coming.

"What makes you so late this morning?" Chris asked.

Louise only shrugged her shoulders. Erik felt the hem of her dress brush his overalls as she sat down to their last meal together. For a long time maybe. They passed food to her.

"Help yourself first," she said to Erik, when he tried to pass her the pancakes.

"Yeah," Chris said. "Better fill up."

"Yes," Julia chimed in. "I was just thinking maybe you should have had a few cooking lessons."

"Oh, he'll make out," Chris said. "Nothing much to it once a feller gits used to it. Except a little monotonous maybe."

"You'll come up here once in a while?" Louise asked quietly.

"Sure he will," her mother said.

"Yeah," Chris insisted.

Talk stopped. Just another meal to get through. They simply passed from one to another–food and broken phrases.

Julia finished first. "More coffee anybody?"

Erik shook his head.

"Naw," Chris said.

Julia stacked her cup and saucer on her plate. Then her silverware. "You mind if I go ahead?" She stood up. "Got a lot to do this morning."

Erik became conscious of the clock, the pendulum swinging behind painted glass, the hard ticking.

"Well." Chris shoved his chair back. "I s'pose we better be goin' then."

Erik stood and Louise glanced up at him, only for an instant. Then she reached for his plate and began to help clear the table.

"Remember to take the box." Julia stood waiting. "It's goodbye then." She held out her hand.

He took it gently, trying to smile as he looked next at Louise, but she already held a stack of dishes in both hands. Why now? "Bye," she said awkwardly.

Erik reluctantly turned away to pick up the carton.

Chris opened the door for him and followed him out. "Here, I'll take that box to the car, while you git your things."

Julia and Louise didn't come out and Erik didn't look back. When Erik got out of the car to open the gate, Chris said, "Just leave it open. I'll be right back."

The brightness of this morning reminded Erik of the morning they drove to the Hills. He had felt sorry for Gus then, staying behind to do the chores. They passed the cornfield and the meadow, where the haystacks stood like markers over the dead summer.

"Nice day," Chris said.

Erik's voice stuck in his throat and he only coughed.

The gate to Gus's field was locked. Gus hadn't closed it all summer; he'd just left it thrown back against the fence. But going away, Gus had thought of it.

"You got the key?" Chris asked.

"He keeps it in his barn."

When Erik came back with it, Chris drove in, Erik picked up his suitcase, and Chris took his two boxes, one under each arm. The hollyhocks by the door leaned brown and dead against the dugout.

"Funny-looking house," Chris remarked. "Ain't it?"

Erik opened the door and held the screen door for Chris.

"Pew," Chris said. "Better git some windows opened." He dropped Erik's boxes on the kitchen table.

Erik tried the window behind the table, but couldn't budge it.

"Hell," Chris said, "he ain't got no screen on it anyhow."

Erik followed him back out to the car.

"I guess it'll be all right when you git it cleaned up a bit." Chris bent to crank his motor. "Well, we'll be seein' you." He got in, sat for a moment looking straight ahead over the hood, and slowly let out the clutch.

Erik watched Chris's car glide out through the field and turn the corner, thin dust rising in the lane. The slats of the open gate made shadows on the ground. Don't think now, Erik told himself. He walked back inside and took his suitcase into Gus's bedroom. Gus's work shoes peeked out from under the bed. Erik moved them into the closet beside a pair of sagging rubber boots. Big-kneed long underwear and baggy overalls hung down over them, and he quickly shut the closet door.

The sod house had no curtains, only a cracked blind over the west window. That sash wouldn't open, but the one on the south window did. Then he returned to the kitchen. He would have to heat water for scrubbing. But first he opened Julia's box.

Inside he found fresh, clean-smelling sheets and a pillow case, with an embroidered "M," to remind him who they belonged to. Lifting the linens out, he uncovered a jar of chokecherry preserves. Instantly he remembered walking down the canyon trail with Julia to pick them–taking such short steps with her. Along the way she'd brought it up about Erik maybe renting Gus's place. He didn't know, he'd said, but he had never doubted how it would turn out.

Erik put away more jars from the box, and a loaf of bread, and some butter. Then he turned to the shabby, streaked mirror hanging over Gus's wash basin. A metal comb with dark hairs lay beside it. The alarm clock had suddenly stopped in the empty house, a little past midnight. Erik slowly wound it, and it began to tick. He would set the time by the afternoon train.

He didn't interrupt his scrubbing to eat at noon. He wasn't hungry, and he would have to wash the dishes first. But when at last he heard the train, he set the alarm clock, and wound it again. To be sure to keep time going.

He still had the strong odor of the scrubbed floor in his nostrils when he went to bed, early. Julia would now be reading aloud the serial in the <u>Ladies Home Journal</u>, with Louise sitting alone in the corner.

A light flickered through the bedroom window–a freight train coming down the flats. He began to hear it, the immense rolling weight bearing down towards him. It moved slowly and made the earth tremble. The windows rattled, and he half sat up in bed. Posts along the track rose sharply out of the darkness and just as quickly disappeared. Finally he could hear only the indistinct, receding roar, toward the creek and through the cut in the tip of the divide.

He dropped back on the bed and after a little became aware of the ticking of the alarm clock in the kitchen. He counted the seconds. One by one. Then hours, days, months, and seasons. Winter first, then spring, and finally summer. Then Gus would return. Gus and his woman. He would bring her here–to this bed.

Erik suddenly felt thirsty, got up, and felt his way—his fingers probing the darkness for the half-open kitchen door. Coals still glowed through the grate of the cookstove. He reached for the match holder and lit a lamp, mainly to push the darkness back while he drank.

But his shadow rose giant-like up the wall onto the ceiling, and he could see his face dimly in the mirror. He stared at it. His reflection looked like Gus for a moment, and he turned quickly to blow out the light. He returned to bed, to sleep and forget. To sleep. Julia's pillowcase smelled clean and sweet, like the sun and the windblown divide.

Yet this long Sunday kept coming back, a bad dream that wouldn't stop. In it he scrubbed the floor again. His knees hurt from it, and he tried to stretch his legs. The thin mattress sagged in the middle, forming the hole in which Gus had lain all these years. Erik stiffened so he wouldn't roll over against him. Gus's heavy limbs felt so close and hairy. His mouth gaped half open, showing his gold crowns, and his rasping snore grew louder.

Erik turned over on his back and was suddenly wide awake. The rasping didn't stop. It came from directly overhead–mice or rats gnawing on the timbers. He could hear one scuttling across the loft.

7

Miss Ainsley ran her fingers over the piano keys. She struck one note several times over, and then the one next to it.

"What's the matter?" Al asked. "Something wrong?"

She glanced up. "Needs tuning."

She was plump, dark, and lively. Erik had seen her before with Al, who had told him she taught grade school, and played the organ on Sundays. Julia had said Miss Ainsley was the reason Al went to church. So Erik wasn't surprised Al had also invited her to his Christmas Eve party.

"Tuning?" Al repeated. "You're kidding. Why it ain't hardly been touched since I got it."

"It gets out of tune anyway just standing there," Julia explained.

"It does?"

Miss Ainsley nodded. "Better have Mr. Wetzel come over. Want me to tell him?"

Al raised his hand as if to ward off evil. "Oh no! Not him! I don't want no more o' that. Why, he was out here right after I got it. Well, if it's out o' tune, I think he's the one that done it. He gave it the works, let me tell you. Why, he'd raise his hands way up and bang down on the keys like the dickens. Just gave it hell, that's all. By golly, the whole room was shakin'. No foolin'! I thought he was gonna pound the front legs through the floor."

Miss Ainsley doubled over laughing.

"You told him off, I s'pose?" Julia egged Al on.

"You darn right I tole him." He glared around the circle. "The bastard."

An abrupt silence fell over them.

Hayden shook his head. "Wrong note."

Miss Ainsley busied herself flipping through pages of music and then struck up with "Jingle Bells," singing it in a teacher's voice.

The rest of the party joined in reluctantly. Besides Miss Ainsley, only Louise and Julia seemed sure of the words.

At the end of the first stanza Miss Ainsley turned around to the rest of them. "Please," she begged.

"Sing you sonofaguns," Al threatened.

Jes moved up behind Louise and her mother, and stretched his scrawny neck like a bird over his stiff collar. Fred stood on the other side of Louise.

"You," Al said to Erik when the music stopped. "Come over here."

Erik shook his head. "I can't sing."

"Sure you can."

"But he doesn't know our carols," Julia protested. "He's never heard them before."

"Don't make no difference."

Miss Ainsley started playing again, and Al sang lustily. His face was flushed from the Christmas spirit, as he called it, which he had brought back from Omaha.

Louise merrily looked up at Fred. How beautiful she looked tonight, Erik thought. He hadn't seen her in such a long time. He had walked to town time and again in the hope of running into her at the store or post office, or on her way to church on Sundays. He knew every culvert, every gate, every clump of weeds along the road. He'd even seen Hayden in his newspaper office.

Miss Ainsley ended with a flourish. "That was fine," she declared.

"Darn right." Al gazed around at everyone happily. "I git a lot o' kick out o' this. Havin' Christmas Eve over here and the house full o' people."

"Shows you what you've been missing all these years," Julia teased.

"You bet."

Chris stood next to his mother's chair, outside the circle by the piano, and he'd kept busy watching the candles on the tree, straightening them, and moving one now and then.

This party reminded Erik of their day in the Hills, with the whole family together. But tonight he didn't expect to get any time alone with Louise, especially with Fred staying so close to her. Perhaps tomorrow he could join her family for dinner and sit next to her. The group at the piano began to break up, the men falling back.

Jes nudged him. "You bring anyt'ing?"

Erik shook his head.

"Naw, dey wouldn't expect it," Jes said.

They both studied the stack of packages under the tree.

Al clapped his hands.

"Where's your red suit, Grandpa?" Louise settled on the piano bench beside Miss Ainsley.

"By golly, it's outgrown him," Al replied. "Just when his beard is gittin' the right color too."

"You're too big a girl for that now." Mayland shifted packages to read their tags.

Erik thought Mayland looked tired and old tonight. How different from an early photograph Erik had seen of him at home–the heroic figure who had lived up to all the expectations for an American immigrant. Including the founding of a city. Folks always talked about Mayland at home. Never about his wife, Martha. Erik had hardly thought of her existence until he met her that first afternoon in her warm, home-like kitchen–with the smell of wood fire and coffee, the tinkling of porcelain and silver, and the familiar idiom of his own language.

Mayland had begun to hand out packages, and Louise proudly held up a silver bracelet.

"How perfectly beautiful!" Julia exclaimed. "He shouldn't have done that."

"Oh, thanks, Fred," Louise cried, her eyes beaming. She stood up and went over to her father to show it to him.

"Aha," he said approvingly.

If only Erik had known about this. He couldn't even make up for it by tomorrow. And he hadn't seen Louise often enough lately to know whether she would want a gift from him. With Fred it was different. They had known each other so long, like cousins.

Jes received a package next, a necktie from Al.

Then Mayland handed a package to Erik, from Louise. She was smiling across to him. He knew what it was before he opened it.

"What is it?" Jes asked.

Erik unwrapped the sketchbook and pencils and showed him.

"What's it for?"

"Drawing." Erik tried to catch her eye, but Louise didn't notice. She was trying to adjust her new bracelet.

Mayland brought Erik another package, and Julia watched him open it. "Give you something to do in your spare time," she said. "If you need a bigger brush, I have one you can use."

"Thanks." Erik tried again to catch Louise's attention with a look, but then Al poked his head in from the dining room.

"Any of you folks wanting to play cards come in here," Al announced.

"All right." Chris got up, and Julia followed him, while Mayland stepped outside.

"What about you fellers?" Al asked Jes and Erik.

"Might as well," Jes said.

Erik packed his new brushes and tubes of watercolor paint back in their box while the party broke into smaller groups. Louise and Fred blew out candles while Miss Ainsley played softly on the piano, and then Fred began to move the chairs back. Erik started to get up to thank Louise, but she walked on over to her grandmother.

Fred stopped to talk with Miss Ainsley. They flipped through the music together, and she began a waltz. Fred promptly beckoned to Louise.

How gracefully she moved to the music, her pumps flickering under her flared skirt. It brushed Erik, and she smiled to him over Fred's shoulder. What a beautiful picture–to capture her like that in the half light! Erik quickly opened his new sketchbook.

He worked rapidly to record what he saw, and checked it again. The image formed magically under his hand: the swirl of her skirt, the position of her feet, the lines of her body and her arms. Then the profile of her head.

Mayland ducked back inside, stamping his feet. "It's beginning to snow."

Fred and Louise stopped, and then also Miss Ainsley.

Al stuck his head in again. "What's that?"

"It's snowing," Mayland repeated.

Al came out of the dining room, followed by Chris, and they went outside together. Fred and Louise walked as far as the door.

Al returned immediately. "By golly, we're gonna have a white Christmas after all, it looks like."

"Is it bad?" Miss Ainsley asked.

"Coming right down, you betcha." Al saw Erik sitting by himself. "You ain't havin' much fun."

Erik looked up from his sketch. "What?"

"You don't sing, you don't dance, you don't play cards. What the devil's the matter with you?"

Erik swallowed. He couldn't ever get used to Al's roughness. Not even as a guest in his home.

Al came closer and noticed his drawing. "So that's what's eatin' you?"

Erik felt a hot surge in his face.

"I thought it damn funny. By God, you better lay off o' her if you know what's best."

Erik slammed his sketchbook shut, gathered up his gifts, and rose instantly.

"What's the matter?" Al gasped, following Erik out. "Can't you take a joke?"

A joke? Erik didn't look back.

They met Chris in the hallway.

"You ain't goin' already?" Al pleaded.

"I think we better," Chris answered, thinking Al's question was meant for him. "Looks like a blizzard to me."

"Holy smokes, the party's only just started."

Erik slapped on his cap, wrapped himself and gifts in his mackinaw, and darted out, stumbling across the yard to

Al's barn. He had to get away, out of sight, out of hearing, before he spoke his anger aloud. He scrambled frantically for his tack, and packed his gifts in his saddlebags. But the sketch pad didn't fit, so he tucked it under his mackinaw, buttoning it closed. He hastily saddled and bridled his mount, one of Gus's work horses, and hauled the reluctant animal outside.

Back in the saddle, Erik could hardly see the road. He lowered his head against stinging particles and pushed Gus's horse into a trot. From his pockets he pulled out his mittens, and fumbled them on in the dark. The wind felt like ice on his legs. The insolence and effrontery of that lout. If Louise had heard Al, she would have told him off. If she found out later . . . they would all know about it. Then how could he face the family again? If there was snow, lots of snow, he wouldn't see any of them for a long time. Not for a very long time. Not that it mattered. Apparently both Julia and Al thought he wasn't good enough for Louise.

Erik had only fence posts to guide him now. What if he got lost? It didn't matter. They knew he didn't want to become an artist. Yet that was all they could think of for Christmas, pushing him to do it. And why hadn't he thought of trying to get some gifts for them?

At last he realized Chris's car was about to overtake him, and he reined his horse to one side. They would see him on the horse, but he wouldn't look at them. The headlights threw his shadow into the drifts and the car swerved past, with its curtains closed and snow swirling in its lights. He watched it drive out of sight–a long white finger in the section lane, moving toward the river.

This was the same road they'd taken to the Hills and back. Erik and Louise had watched the sun dip down below the peaks and then they had returned home in the darkness, closer together than they had ever been before or since. Now she'd probably just passed by in the curtained car without ever thinking of him or that day.

Erik pushed his sketch pad farther up under his mackinaw. He held his mittened hand against the side of his face and then over his nose. He'd get even colder when he turned north. He whimpered aloud. He'd have no place to stop once he passed through town. He just needed to get back into Gus's sod house and let it close in over him.

Suddenly Erik felt like somebody was following him. Was it just the wind he heard, whining and driving snow through weeds and fences? Or was it a team, another saddle horse, or somebody else going home? He tried to urge his horse into a trot again, but it lowered its head doggedly.

Erik heard a voice and looked back.

"Why didn't you tell me you was leaving?" Jes called, urging his mount to catch up.

"Oh," Erik said.

"Wish I'd left the cows in."

"Yes?"

"Some is gonna have calves damit."

Erik opened his lips, but had no answer.

"Why don't you come up in de holidays?" Jes rode up alongside. "Gits so damn lonely."

"Yes." It sounded like the icy wind through his teeth.

"You do dat," Jes repeated. "You ain't seen my new shack yet."

When the Ice went out in Febr.

Erik saw the lights from town and then the steel bridge across the river. The wind wasn't so strong here in the shelter of the slope, but he could hear the limbs of the cottonwoods creaking.

Jes and Erik parted in town, Jes to ride west and Erik east. Erik goaded his horse into a trot again through the empty street, up over the track, and down the section lane across the flats. He felt numbed clear through. At last he slid stiffly to the ground in front of Gus's barn and stumbled through it in the dark, struggling just to get the horse in its stall, unsaddled, unbridled, and partly groomed.

As soon as he entered the front room of Gus's sod house and shut the door on the storm, he thankfully found the kitchen still warm. He had brought in his saddlebags. He shed his mittens, unbuttoned his mackinaw, and unloaded his gifts on the kitchen table. He warmed his hands over the stove and lit the lamp, its yellow light reflecting on the window panes. Finally he removed his jacket and began to undress, as he moved into the cold bedroom. To sleep and forget. To not feel or be. He lay listening to the creaking rafters, as the wind filled the night and Dakota with snow.

Erik lay watching while dawn began to light his quilt. Snow stung the window behind him, and he turned to watch. It soon covered the panes, as if someone had pulled a sheet over them. And the memory of last night overtook him like a recurrent pain. It wasn't only what Al had said which haunted Erik now, but also his own sulking and leaving in a huff. And now, on Christmas Day, last night was all he had to think about. Snow would block the roads, so he couldn't ride up to Chris's even if he wanted to.

He slid from under his covers and hurried to the kitchen to start a fire, soaking the kindling with kerosene. For a moment he couldn't tell whether the roar he heard was his fire or the wind in the chimney. Snow had sifted under the front door and against a gunnysack he had spread on the floor, to wipe his feet on. He discovered ice in the water pail, and the clock had stopped again.

Erik rushed to dress by the stove and then opened the door, wind and snow lashing through, sending the gunnysack sailing across the floor. Outside he could barely see the barn, and he waded in snow hip-deep to the corral gate.

Gus's cattle stood huddled in the corral, waiting to be fed. When they saw him they began bawling. He tried to close the corral gate, but the snow was too deep. He would have to fetch the scoop. So he climbed onto the snow-draped stack first. It stood on the north side, forming a windbreak for the corral. He tore through the icy crust with a pitchfork until he found a layer of hay to peel off–a buried layer of summer. The wind helped carry the hay over the fence, and the cattle mauled each other getting to it.

Erik quickly returned to the dugout for the saddlebags, and then went back outside to return them to the barn, shivering hard as he ducked into the drafty barn. It felt just as cold inside. The horses stood hunched up, and whinnied impatiently. He fed them and cleaned their stalls, while he tried to ignore a constant banging overhead. But at last he climbed a ladder, and found a door in the west gable had blown open. After fastening it closed, he climbed back down, retrieved the scoop, and went back outside to get the corral gate closed. Finally all he had left to do was carry in firewood.

Once the kitchen warmed up, he started breakfast. For a little he had forgotten his pain. Whenever he had duties he found he could lose himself in them. A spot began to melt in the middle of the window. He could see cottonwoods swaying. The snow was letting up, for the moment at least. If only he could have work he liked, as the others did.

Erik guessed it would look like the snowy morning all day, until the sky grew dark again. Louise would sit in the parlor and also watch the snow–enveloped spruce, teased by the breath of the Hills. The wood fire would glow behind the isinglass and reflect in the china cabinet.

Why had Louise acted so distant since Erik left? Had she never forgiven him for leaving without warning–without even fighting this move to Gus's? Would it ever be the same between them again?

Erik reached for his new sketchbook and looked at the lines he couldn't stop himself from drawing. Just a beginning–the back of her head with the twin knots of her braids, her neckline, her puffed sleeves and her shoulders. His lines converged at her waist and then swirled out–as if she would turn in an instant and show her face. Al had recognized her at once. "So that's what's eatin' you!"

That big bully! Al couldn't understand this dancing on paper, but he knew what it meant. Why was he so concerned, anyway? Why did he care?

Was it his adopted son, after all? But didn't Fred have a girl out north? He hadn't said anything about her for a long time. Erik had meant to ask, in fact had the question ready when Fred came to invite him to Al's party. But Erik hadn't asked. By then it had seemed too late, if it was an answer he didn't want to hear.

It had nearly stopped snowing when he finished breakfast, and he realized he was again trying to confine a part of the divide through a window pane. His eyes followed the thin line where sky and wind hit the rim. And he stood up to look for a larger pad of paper in the front room.

He found the front room had more light, with hardly any frost on the windows, but it felt icy cold. Out the windows lay only whiteness for as far as he could see. The wind swept its frozen breath over long running drifts, ditches, and the railroad embankment with its stiff telegraph poles, like white crosses in the right-of-way. A wail reached him before it blew away, and the morning freight train slowly pushed its white nose through. After it passed, his mind still drifted over the cold fields until he began to shiver. Then he remembered why he'd come in here.

Erik retrieved the large pad of paper Hayden had given him one Sunday afternoon when he was out for a walk in town, looking for Louise, as usual. Hayden had beckoned Erik into his office, shifted papers on his desk, and found the pad for Erik. Hayden had told Erik he'd had it a long time, having once toyed a little with drawing cartoons. Hayden had talked a long time, not about art, but about early days in Dakota and gold mining in the Hills.

Erik had finally said, "You know words, right?"

"Sure." Hayden had chuckled.

"What does honyockers mean?"

"Who said that to you?" Hayden abruptly sounded fierce.

"Al said it, about people out north."

"Al said it?" Hayden had suddenly laughed. "Son, let me give you some advice. Don't ever say that word again." Hayden had noticed Erik's puzzled look. "I laughed because Al is the son of Honyockers, which is an insulting word for Scandinavian immigrants."

Erik's face had burned. Honyocker. Erik suddenly wondered if that was why Julia and Al thought he wasn't good enough for Louise. How insulting!

Erik shook his head at the memory, and set the pad from Hayden on the kitchen table. He washed his dishes, while remembering a late afternoon he had ridden to town for the mail, more, as always, in the hope of seeing Louise. She hadn't come. Instead he had called for Chris's mail, so he could take it out to their house. Erik would also help with the chores, and they might ask him to stay for supper. But he'd found no one home.

Then he rode back over the divide, crossing the unclaimed homestead. And he had sat here afterward, staring through the window pane and tried to sketch the divide on the pad–what he could see of it. Darkness came, but he had tried again–just to pass the time. Time ran so fast whenever he drew or painted. But again he had not succeeded. His inability to capture the divide on paper had troubled him more than he wanted to admit.

Now he sat back down at the table after finishing his dishes, and leafed through his many sketches of the divide, but they still all looked the same–not like the divide, but more like a familiar hill behind the trees, the kind he had often drawn at home. And it wasn't as if he didn't know the divide. Day in and day out he stared up at it, lying there with its gullied face to the sun and wind. He didn't even have to look at it to see it. It was always there. As a boy he had read a story about a prince setting out to find the end of the world. Erik had imagined the prince's goal as a bleak and sterile slope, like the divide, where the earth disappeared into space.

The divide was lonely, unfenced, and unwanted. It possessed hardly any lines. He studied one of his sketches more closely. It was made of lines, lines like his drawing of the church, lines to limit and separate, to hold objects in their places. Was that his problem? Had he tried to hold the divide down? Had he felt unable to release it? Just as he was unable to let go of the idea of the homestead, let go of all this Dakota life that he wanted to give himself up to? He hadn't expected to want to stay here. It was just a place to start. But its terrible beauty kept tugging at him.

He got up again to warm his fingers over the stove, all the while looking out. Snow now covered up details and distractions. Only the elemental remained: the ghostly swaying cottonwoods, and the white-sheeted slope heading up and up to the blurred margins of wind, snow, and cloud.

Erik suddenly realized this would have to be a painting, not a drawing. He cleared the table and mounted a sheet on the stiff cover of the paper pad. The nostalgic smell of paint carried him back to all he had once cared for. He wiped the window pane clean and propped up his pad. Then he became all nerves, unmindful of anything but the scene through the window. Tree trunks with bare limbs first formed the foreground along the creek, and next loomed the divide.

Erik had lost track of the time when he at last stepped back to study his painting from the door to Gus's bedroom. Except for the cottonwoods Erik could turn the picture upside down without changing anything–anything that mattered. Only the point of view would alter–to a foreground of cloud rising toward the white slopes of the earth. The sky and earth stood together equal, one as good as the other.

He put more wood in the stove and returned to his task. As more of the divide emerged under his brush, cold and aloof, solid earth under snow, he experienced again the secret thrill he'd almost forgotten. Yet he also felt something new this time, something he had not known before. This time he'd gone beyond mere surface or romantic escape, but to find the full depth of it–a divide of Dakota as it would remain after the snow melted, after he was gone.

Erik squinted against the glare of sun and snow as his mount reached the top of the draw. Jes's dugout had partly collapsed and disappeared under the snow. Jes's new shack stood naked and unpainted in the frozen whiteness. Wood smoke rising from the flue provided the only sign of life. The shack possessed no north windows, only a door, a little off center.

Erik could see the river below, and the gaunt cottonwoods on both sides stood singularly clear and distinct, like a stereopticon slide. Beyond rose the foothills and the dazzling slopes of the mountains. He sat still in his saddle for a moment, admiring their shimmering beauty. The mountains seemed closer today. Colors would change and the valley deepen as the sun sank, but the mountains would be visible into night. He returned his gaze to the single file of fence posts, knee-deep in snow, with their sharp blue shadows.

Erik rode down to the corral, tied his horse to the fence, and walked up to the shack door. He could hear sawing inside and he knocked loudly, rattling the door in its latch.

The sawing stopped and Jes opened his door. "Oh, it's you. Come in."

The shack had only one room, over three by four meters, unfinished like Erik's woodshed. The stovepipe stuck straight up through a square hole in the roof. Jes had been sawing firewood by the stove. "It's a helluva mess," Jes apologized.

Erik began to shed his mittens, cap, and mackinaw.

"Put 'em on the cot dere," Jes said, "and come over here with me by the stove." He finished sawing the wood he'd started, poked the piece he sawed off into the stove, and sat on his stool by his wood box.

"Ya," Jes said. "Had the damndest luck dis Christmas. Lost tree calves."

Erik pulled up a chair.

"Had to come in dis blizzard, Godamit."

Erik nodded sympathetically. "At least you saved your stove and your cot."

"But tree dead calves. Sonsobitses."

"What?"

"Sonsobitses, I said."

"Oh?"

"I guess you been in dis country long enough to know what that is."

Erik smiled weakly. "No." He looked at Jes. "I don't know." Another strange word.

"You mean you ain't heard it before?"

"Sure. I guess so." But that wasn't the way Chris pronounced it. "What does it mean?"

"Just a cuss word. I mean, for the cows."

"But what does it mean?"

"Damn if I know. What's the difference? Ask Lou–ask Fred, I mean."

Talk came to a halt for a moment.

"Gittin' purdy t'ick with Louise, ain't he?"

Erik felt his face redden. "Fred's got a girl out north."

"He does?"

Erik nodded.

"The hell. I didn't know that. I'll hafto kid him about it, the sonofabits."

"I don't know if he wanted me to tell," Erik said hastily, wishing he'd kept quiet.

"Hell, he don't care." Jes got up. "I'm gonna make some coffee."

Erik stood up too. The sun glared though the front windows. Jes's new shack had no curtains or blinds. "Got a good view here."

"Ya, it's all right." Jes stepped outside for a moment to fill a pail with snow and then plunked it on the stove, which was red hot. "I sometimes wonder if it's worth it," he added. "Hafto saw all the time just to keep from freezin' to death. Godamit, li'ble to lose ever't'ing anyway."

Erik didn't answer. What could he say?

"We're just a couple damn fools, I guess," Jes continued. "I dunno. Sometimes I wish I was dead." He looked pitifully at Erik. "That's a helluva way to feel, ain't it? But it's the truth. It gits so Godam lonesome. But what's you gonna do? You can't go back. You ever t'ink you'll go back sometime?"

Erik shook his head.

"Your folks dead, ain't they?"

"My mother is."

"Oh ya, I remember. It's your stepmother that's related to Mayland, ain't she? Naw, I don't wanta go back either. The folks ain't got nothing. Just workin' on a dairy. Course, they t'ink I'm sittin' purdy here with a farm o' my own."

Another silence ensued, as if they'd come to the end of their thoughts. Jes poured melted snow-water into his coffee pot, and found a cup for Erik, wiping the rim with his thumb. He glanced up.

"I seen your drawing Mr. Hayden put in the paper."

"Oh?"

"You done some in the old country Mrs. Mayland says. Done any in the book you got yet?"

"Not much. I also did a watercolor," Erik added quickly, not wanting to talk about his sketch of Louise, or the drawings he'd done to make time go away at Gus's, during the snowed-in days after the watercolor. Work-scuffed shoes, old rubber boots, sagging saddlebags, and cold work horses in their stalls. Anything he'd started in the drafty barn, he'd finished in the warm kitchen. Nothing important. Jes wouldn't understand.

"Ya." Jes poured the coffee. "What's that?"

Erik tried to explain his watercolor.

"Ya. Vel, I don't know nothing about it. Not much in it, I guess."

Erik sipped his hot coffee.

"In dis country anyway," Jes continued. "You can buy 'em cheap, least the printed kind. And they're purdier too if you ask me. Like that calendar." Jes nodded at the glossy girl with the cream separator Erik had seen in his dugout. "Ain't she purdy?"

"Aha." So Jes had rescued her too.

"But I s'pose there must be somet'ing I don't 'preciate."

Erik studied the print. "Nobody looks like that."

"No, maybe not. What's the difference if she's purdy?"

"It isn't the truth."

"Da truth, ha? Hell, I already got too much o' that. I want something to forget it." Jes paused. "What was it you painted?"

"Just the crick and the divide."

"Ya? I wouldn't t'ink anybody'd care for that?"

"No-o," Erik conceded. "I just wanted to, I guess." He was about to say "had to," but he again realized Jes wouldn't understand.

"Vel, don't pay no attention to me," Jes said.

Erik tried to think of something else to talk about.

"Maybe I'll come by and see your painting sometime," Jes added.

"I don't have it anymore. Mr. Hayden sent it away."

"He did? What for?"

"To enter it into an art exhibit back east."

"That so?"

Erik peered up at the opening around the flue.

"Ya, I didn't git it fixed in time. It's too damn cold now."

Their talk veered to the building of the shed and Jes's plans for the future.

"Kinda tough right now, but I'll pull through, I guess," Jes concluded.

Erik watched the sun sinking in the west window and rose to go.

"I hafto go too," Jes said. "Time to start my chores." He picked up one coat inside another, as he'd shed them. His shabby outer jacket had a side pocket ripped down the seam, and it hung like a flap, exposing the lining.

They walked together into frozen stillness. The sun stared coldly from the rim of the plateau. Jes started down the draw toward his cowshed, and Erik headed down to his horse humped up by the corral fence. Erik's breath steamed white. He untied his horse and swung into the saddle. Darkness would descend before he got home.

Erik rode uphill at first, and when he turned east he could make out Broken Rock on the horizon. How small it looked from here, as if in a painting. That was the way he should remember it. This day would just become another memory, like home. That was the truth.

Suddenly a sharp cry pierced right through him. The coyote cried again, and more joined in, their singing sustained and lonely. He jarred his horse into a trot through the crunching snow.

Evening filled the basin as he reached it. He had ridden this way the first time last spring, on Louise's mount. She had offered to loan Brownie to Erik because he was a gentle pony. It was just after the runaway. She had made the offer because she was gentle. Was she lost to him now? Without her, life had little meaning for him here. From the north slopes of the knolls he watched the yellow light in her house. The woodshed stood cold and empty now. As the house light passed from sight, he descended into the flats he knew so well.

Gus sent Erik a postcard, a group snapshot in front of a cottage. Gus had marked an X above the girl standing next to him. Her name was Anna, he wrote. Erik took the card to show Chris's family, but they already had one too.

"Well, he didn't lose much time," Julia commented. "I hope she knows what she's getting into. I sure don't envy her."

"Looks like a nice girl," Chris said.

"It's a dirty shame," Julia said.

"Oh, I don't know," Chris replied. "He ain't so bad. Once she gits the place cleaned up."

Louise turned to Erik. "You coming back here then?"

He glanced at Chris. "I don't know–if you want me."

"Sure," Chris said.

"Look at him all dressed up, fit to kill," Julia added, still studying the picture.

Erik helped with the chores and stayed for supper.

"Yeah," Chris said when Erik was ready to go, "there'll be enough to do this fall. I figger maybe we'll feed the cattle right here on the crick next winter. Might as well. It shouldn't take a helluva lot to fix the woodshed. Just a layer o' tarpaper, I guess."

The long winter finally showed signs of letting go of Dakota. The last of the snowdrifts melted along the ditches, and the spring winds began to blow. Erik was looking across at the empty homestead again, and one day he hinted about it to Chris.

"Yeah, it wouldn't be bad," Chris said. "Fred was thinking of takin' it once, but I guess he's figgerin' on gittin' a place out north. He don't like farmin'. More like Al that way."

Erik felt his heart lighten. He knew Louise wanted to stay close to home. But he said nothing more about the homestead then. Instead he returned to it many times to look it over. He made plans and sketches of the shack and the barn and of where he'd dig the ditches. And one day when he was in town he stopped by the lumberyard to get some estimates. He was just thinking about it, he was careful to say. He would also need a team, he realized, and a wagon and tools. But by the end of the summer, or at least in a year, he should have nearly enough money saved up.

He had almost forgotten about his watercolor when Hayden mentioned it. They met on the street that day.

"Say, I've been meaning to tell you it came back quite a while ago," Hayden apologized. "I thought I might send it on to another exhibit sometime."

"Oh, it doesn't matter," Erik answered. "I guess it isn't very good."

"I think that one was quite good. But you never can tell what will be accepted," Hayden said. "Of course, you have to keep trying."

"What did they say?" Erik found he couldn't help asking. "Did they say anything?"

"Naw, your painting got there too late, it seems. They didn't have room for it. Something like that. 'Course, they get a lot of pictures. More than they can use. From all over the country. I just happened to see their notice and thought it wouldn't hurt to send it in."

"Oh."

"You want to come by and pick it up sometime?"

Erik nodded.

"I wouldn't give up though," Hayden added hastily. "Try something else maybe."

"I don't know," Erik said evasively. His work had never been accepted before. Why should it be any different now?

"Ever tried a portrait?" Hayden persisted.

"Oh. I guess so. A long time ago."

"They don't want landscapes so much, it seems. Get so many of 'em, you know."

Erik nodded again, anxious to go.

"Of course, I s'pose it wouldn't hurt to also learn a little more about it if you have the time. Ever thought of going to art school? It takes a long time, I guess, to become really good at it."

"Yes," Erik agreed. "I've never really been interested enough."

Hayden just looked at him.

"I mean, not for a long time."

"Well, it's something you can't push, I guess." Hayden turned to go. "I'll be seeing you."

Erik tried to convince himself that he felt only relief about his painting. That he wouldn't have to feel uncertain about what he wanted to do. And the more he thought about it, the more sure he became that Hayden hadn't said all he knew. Erik could at least have the comfort of knowing he wasn't any good at art even if he wanted to be. He could forget all about it then, and concentrate on the rest of his life. But he felt surprisingly let down just the same, and the thought of it kept haunting him. If only he didn't have to spend so much time alone, dwelling on it without anyone to talk to.

It was still too early for spring work, but Chris now had to haul hay from the lower meadow. One afternoon when he needed to attend a meeting of the Irrigators' Association, he drove by to ask Erik to bring up a load for the feeding racks.

Erik drove a hayrack into the yard just as Louise rode home from school. Brownie saw the hay and followed Erik's load up to the feeding racks.

"That isn't fair," Louise objected.

"Everything is fair in love and war," Erik replied from the top of his wagon load.

"Well, you come down here and I'll tend to you."

"All right." But he defied her by climbing down over the back end. In doing so, he nearly dislodged a wad of hay. He glanced uneasily back up at it.

Louise rode over, rose instantly in her stirrups to touch it, and it cascaded down over him. He came out blowing and sputtering.

She slid off her pony and started to run, but he quickly caught her. "You started it."

"I can kick, you know," she threatened, "or scream."

He didn't let go, and after a little she stopped straining against him. "What do you want?"

"Lou-ise."

"We mustn't stay here," she whispered, prying at his arm.

"It's been so long," he started again.

She abruptly stiffened, and he glanced up and felt limp all over. Chris stood in the barn doorway, and looked right at them.

It felt like an eternity before Chris spoke. "I thought maybe you'd like to stay for supper."

Erik nodded, stood there like a foolish culprit, and wished he could think of something to say.

"You better go and help Mama, Louise, hadn't you?" Chris added, and returned inside the barn as if nothing had happened.

"I didn't hear him," Louise whispered. "Did you?"

"He must have been there the whole time."

"Yeah, I guess so. I guess I better go."

Erik stood dumbly watching Louise walk away, his heart pounding.

"Oh," she called back to him. "I forgot about Brownie. Will you put him away for me?"

"Sure."

And he rushed to do it and unload the hay, feeling empty inside, until he could follow her into the house.

8

Summer was dry. The sparse slopes above the ditch looked bare and drab. On hot nights when Erik drove a team back to Gus's from work at Chris's, he could see Mat Burk's horses desperately trying to catch a breeze on the bald tops of knolls. They stood darkly etched against the sky.

The second cutting of alfalfa went into full swing. Once again Erik could sit with Louise in the shade of the stack after lunch, while Chris took his nap.

"I like the smell." Louise turned her face to the stack. "Don't you?"

Erik forgot to answer, watching her, daydreaming about her.

"Don't you?" she repeated, giving him a shove. He caught her wrist, glancing toward Chris lying near the other end of the stack, his hat over his face.

She tried to free herself, but not very hard, and he caught her other wrist.

"Remember the other time," she said, barely moving her lips, also glancing in her father's direction.

"Ever say anything?"

She shook her head and started pulling again.

"Louise."

She looked at him with her blue eyes. "You like to say that, don't you?"

"You think you could ever . . ."

She lowered her eyes, and he wavered momentarily.

"You think," he started over.

"You want to know something?" she said.

"Yes," he said eagerly.

"I'm going away."

"Away?" He felt blood draining from his face.

"To college." She dropped her hands to her lap, with him still holding on. "Mamma thinks I should." She looked at him again. "It's only up to the Hills."

His eyes followed the beautiful lines of her body to her bare ankles. Could he remember them long enough for a portrait? He hadn't brought his sketch pad.

"I'll–" she stopped. Chris stirred, and she took her hands back from Erik. "It isn't for quite a while yet," she added matter-of-factly. Of course not. She'd probably have to leave in the fall, right about the time Erik would be free of Gus's place. Erik looked away in lonely silence. How long did college last here?

Meanwhile work continued. After the haying Erik cut barley and then wheat. Round and round he drove the binder over the baked gumbo and jarring ditches, with the smell of machine oil and the heavy sweetness of ripe grain in his nostrils. Day after day felt the same in the burning sun. Each night after supper at Chris's, Erik drove the hayrack back through the breaks and down the dusty lanes to the dark sod house, with mosquitoes whining on the screen door.

But the day Erik could leave Gus's came at last, a bright still morning like the day Chris had brought him. Erik loaded his belongings in the hayrack, and made a last round through the house. Then he slowly closed the door on his memories, his many lonely days, meals by himself, hours by the window looking across at the homestead and the divide, his ceaseless longing, and his thoughts of this moment. After he drove the hayrack through the gate, he got down and locked it. He took the key to its rusty nail in the barn. Then he climbed the gate and onto the hayrack, with Prince eager to go and Sally lagging a little behind.

Chris met Gus and his bride at the train station and brought them home with him for supper. Al came over too. Gus was all smiles and better dressed than Erik had ever seen him before. His bride looked much younger, a yellow-haired buxom country girl.

"I'm gonna have you folks over too," Al said. "Soon as you git settled." He nodded and smiled at Gus's bride, who didn't understand a word. "Annie, that's her name, ain't it?"

"Anna," Gus corrected.

"Ya," she turned to Gus, misunderstanding.

"Yeah," Al continued. "I was gonna say she'll hafto take the place of Lou' now. You know she's goin' away, Gus?"

"Ya?"

"To college, by golly!"

"Yumping Uniper."

"Jupiter, you mean, Gus?" Julia said. "Don't you?"

"Yupiter or Yuniper, vat's the difference?"

"Naw, I guess there ain't much," Al agreed.

"It's only a leetle vile since you started to school," Gus said. "I vas building the house den."

"You remember taking her to school a good many times," Julia said.

"You bet," Gus said.

Al offered to drive Gus and Anna home when they were ready to go.

"Well, I think she's very nice," Julia said after they'd gone.

"Yeah," Chris agreed. "Seems like a nice girl. Oughta be quite a help to him."

"Clean, anyway," Julia added.

"Must be hard not to understand anything," Chris said.

"How's she going to learn?" Louise asked.

The next Sunday was Louise's last before going away, and she went the rounds with her family to say goodbye. It was nice, Julia said, that they had Erik there again to do the chores. They didn't know when they'd get back. "It might be late," she added.

After they left, Erik noticed buffalo berries growing bright red like fresh droplets of blood along the creek, and overhead glossy cottonwood leaves turned in the breeze like spangles. But the heavy corral posts threw dark bars on the ground. Pungent manure with cattle tracks in it lay scattered everywhere, and yellow straws glistened in the sun. The shadow on the end of the barn moved out like a thin wedge. He walked to the woodshed and sat on the bed to mope.

The next morning Erik drove Louise's trunk in the lumber wagon to the train station. He felt like he was delivering a coffin. And when he rose from the noon meal, Louise followed him to the door.

"I guess I better say goodbye now." She held her hand out to him.

Erik's hand was chapped, and he hadn't washed the grease from the binder off it. He took her hand awkwardly.

"Maybe someday you'll need to leave this place too," Louise said.

"You're letting the flies in," Julia called out musically, before Erik could ask Louise what she meant. They let the screen door slam closed between them, and the sun shone bright in Erik's eyes. He didn't see Louise again that day, but he watched her train from the field. For quite a while he could also hear the wheels rolling, the sound carried so far in the still afternoon.

Erik stood beside the shaking grain separator and pitched bundles over the flapping drive belt. One after another they slid through hacking knives into the screaming cylinder. Grain poured clean and heavy into waiting box wagons, and straw and chaff belched in the sun over the blown rim of the mounting yellow drift. The men peered out of dust-bearded faces and communicated with signs and shouts. And through it all thumped the iron heart of the engine.

They washed before meals outside the kitchen door with loud laughter and nose blowing, and then went inside to eat heartily. Sharp barley spears scratched them through their underwear and stabbed through their socks. Chores got done late and the light in the kitchen stayed on even later. When Erik finally dropped into bed each night, the threshing machine reappeared in his dreams and he worked all night. He awoke each morning more tired than ever.

Yet the end of the threshing at Chris's brought no respite, for then they had to go the rounds to help the neighbors in turn.

Erik and Chris returned home unusually late one night. They had helped finish a job by lantern light because it looked like rain soon, and then while moving to the next place, the machine had bogged down in a field where irrigation water had spilled. Chris and Julia had already gone to bed, and as Erik was undressing, he suddenly heard a rider coming in at a gallop. Erik pushed his screen door open and looked out. Gus slid down from his saddle.

"She's sick," Gus gasped on Erik's steps. "Git the doctor quick. She's out of her head."

Erik grabbed his pants. "I'll go get Chris."

"I had to leave her," Gus whimpered in his doorway. "She's out of her head!"

Erik shoved his shoes on. "Yes, you go on back to her. We'll come. Right away."

Gus sobbed aloud in the darkness and shuffled back down the steps.

Erik ran as he was, his shoe laces flapping. He could hear Gus cutting across the creek on his horse.

"Erik can take me over to Gus's," Julia said to Chris, "while you get the doctor."

Erik hurried back out to the barn. When he led the harnessed and hitched team out, Chris's car was already racing through the breaks, and a short while later headlights streaked across the bottoms.

Julia climbed up beside Erik on the spring seat. "She's going to have a baby. I'm afraid that's what it is. Coming too soon."

"She wasn't feeling right when she helped with the threshers," Julia added after a while. "Neither of them knew about it, of course. He's so dumb. She hadn't even seen a doctor."

Erik drove home alone after the doctor came. He went straight to bed and lay listening for the car. When he woke up, it was raining. The car hadn't come. He ate breakfast, did chores alone, and then returned to the woodshed. It was nearly noon before he heard the car drive up. He came out to find out what happened. Julia went directly to the house.

"Anna's dead," Chris said. "Never came out of the anesthetic."

They buried Anna on the hill above town, in a plot Mayland had donated when the town site was staked out. She was first to be buried there. Gus had paid for a funeral home and coffin, Chris drove it up to the plot on his sleigh, and several men, including Gus, had worked hard to dig her grave. Erik had stayed away from the funeral and the cemetery, not wanting to chance seeing Anna's dead body.

Gus stayed at Al's through the weeks that followed. The last thing Gus did before he left was to have a small granite marker placed on Anna's grave. The bank took his place, which he'd mortgaged, first for his trip and again for the funeral.

Chris and Erik tarpapered the woodshed. It reminded Erik of a casket studded with bright nails.

Julia took Anna's death harder than Erik would have expected. Often they ate meals now in a dead silence. Chris would gaze at her at times, as if hoping for a sign of her former self. They hardly ever went to church now either. Perhaps Julia was missing Louise too, Erik thought, but one noon on their way to the barn, Chris dropped a hint about another reason.

"Julie frets over the way it happened. She had to help with the anesthetic. There wasn't anybody else. I wish somebody could tell her it wasn't her fault. She was only doin' what the doctor told her."

Erik took to helping Julia with the dishes when he could.

"I'm glad you're here," she finally said one day. "It gets so lonesome here all day."

One day he showed her his painting.

"It's a lonesome place," she said. "Isn't it?"

He couldn't meet her eyes.

"You made it down there." She meant Gus's place. After a little pause, she added "I wonder where he is."

Erik began to regret bringing the watercolor. She was still looking at it.

"I guess mine aren't much good. Just silly little things. I couldn't do anything like this, I know. Why don't you go on with it?"

"Oh," he answered evasively, "I have enough to do."

"I wonder if you aren't wasting your time here."

"No," he said. "I don't think so. I like it here."

She looked at him as he thought she had never looked at him before. Impulsively he put his arm around her shoulder, and she pulled her handkerchief out of her apron pocket to wipe her eyes. "I don't know what's the matter with me. I don't know why I should feel this way. It's silly."

"Would you let me make a drawing of you?" he asked suddenly.

"Why?"

"I'd sure like to."

"I don't know why you would." She kept rubbing her eyes as if to erase what had happened. "If you want to," she said.

He set up for it in her kitchen on Thanksgiving afternoon. Chris had gone over to his folks. Julia sat near the window, where the north light lit her face and the slope of the divide showed through the panes. She got up to look at his work from time to time, but said very little.

When they finally stopped due to darkness, she said, "I'd like for Mr. Hayden to see it."

Erik nodded.

"I can see it looks like me, all right. I guess I'm getting older."

He began to pack up.

"I never expected to have my picture made," she added. "I don't know why you wanted to do it." She continued to look at him as if for an answer.

He shook his head, not knowing the answer himself.

"I've had a lot on my mind this fall," she said. "It seems I've had to bear more than I could sometimes."

"Yes." He didn't know what else to say.

She gazed at him, puzzled. "We just do our best, I guess. That's all we can do."

Snow arrived for this Christmas, not like the year before, but soft and flaky. It festooned brambles and bushes along the creek, and flung white streamers down the limbs of the cottonwoods, where sunlight normally gleamed. The snow made the trains late, so Mayland arranged to meet Louise and take her home with him. Erik would take the sleigh to pick her up from Mayland's before supper.

The clouds began to lift in the afternoon, and when Erik and Louise started home after dark, the sky was clear and cold.

"Grandma is wonderful, isn't she?" Louise said, as they rode up the curve. "Always the same."

Erik nodded.

"She hasn't had a very easy life either."

"No-o."

The town with its white roofs and lighted windows seemed as still as a picture.

Louise looked off toward the hill. "That's where she's buried, isn't it? Anna, I mean."

"Yes."

"And Gus has left."

Sally was lagging behind, and Erik slapped her with the line.

"Anybody heard from him?"

Erik shook his head. "No, I guess not. He was thinking of going back to the Hills. He worked in the mines once, when he first came over."

They passed the church and turned north. The sleigh runners made light thumps and the links of the traces tinkled in the quiet air.

"Mamma took it pretty hard, didn't she?"

Erik nodded in the semi-darkness.

"Papa can stand it better. Because he's a man, I guess."

Again Erik nodded.

"I remember when I was little, and cried over something, he'd always say, 'You got to be tough.'" Louise looked at Erik. "You think that's something you can learn?"

"I don't know."

"I don't think so. He isn't really very tough, is he?" And after a little she added, "I think maybe that's why he said it."

The sleigh bumped over the tracks and began the ascent.

"Mamma wrote you made a picture of her."

"Ye-es. A drawing."

"And Mr. Hayden sent it to Chicago."

"Ye-es."

"Ever hear from them about it?"

"No. Not yet." Driving the same road tonight, Erik thought about his ride with Chris his first night here.

Louise tightened the robe over their laps and slid closer. "Mr. Hayden seems to think your drawing's pretty good, and that you ought to go to art school. I sure wish I could see Mamma's portrait."

"I'd rather talk about you," Erik tried to counter.

"Why?"

"Oh because."

"Because what?"

"You know."

"Ha. Why is it people can never say what they mean but just have to hint at it?"

"Yes–sweetheart."

She shoved his arm with her mittened hand, and he tried to grab her hand.

"Watch your driving," she warned.

He looked at her. "Where did you get your red mittens?"

"A store near school. You like 'em?"

"Yes. I like everything you get."

The basin and the flats appeared over the hill, a white expanse to the edge of darkness.

"You remember the rides in the rain last year?" she said.

He nodded, smiling, and then came a silence broken only by the horses as they started trotting downhill, to the embankment at the base of the first knoll.

"You remember," he finally said, as they slowed for the culvert, "you didn't like it."

"Didn't like it?" she repeated.

"Well, you said you didn't like it when it was rainy. You said you couldn't stand it."

"I don't remember that. I know I didn't mean it. I think I've always liked it here. When did I say that?"

"Oh, one day, don't you remember?"

"No." She shook her head. "I don't remember that. I know I didn't mean it. I s'pose I like it better when it's sunny. But it can't be all the time. I know that."

He nodded.

"No," she continued. "You can't imagine how many times I've thought of this, coming home again, and driving down this road. I could just cry."

He turned toward her.

"I s'pose you think that's silly."

"No," he said softly.

"I can't help it."

He waited a little. "Don't you like it? College, I mean."

"Oh, it's all right."

There was another pause.

"I don't care for it too much," she finally admitted.

"You're going back, though?" Erik bit his lip.

"Oh sure, I'll go back, all right. This year, anyway."

They reached the top of the knolls, and could see the light from the house.

"It's going to be harder to leave this time, I'm afraid," she said. "But it isn't so long till spring, is it?"

"No-o," Erik lied. "It isn't so very long."

Louise tugged at the robe again and bent toward him to tuck it under.

"You know," he said, taking a deep breath, "I've been thinking of taking up that homestead across the crick."

"Oh?"

"You remember the first time we went over there together?"

"No. When was that?"

"Don't you remember?" he said, not knowing whether to feel disappointment or relief. "The time I got dizzy on the flume," he admitted.

"Oh!" She laughed. "Yes, I remember."

"I can walk on it now."

She looked towards the homestead.

"You said maybe you'd take it," he reminded her.

"Well, I'll come down and see you."

"Will you?" he asked, with too much eagerness.

"Sure," she said.

"Is that all?" he said, hiding sadness in his voice.

She leaned past him, and evaded his question. "I can't see any light down there. Nobody living in Gus's house?"

"No," he answered, anxious to get back to his line of thought. But suddenly they saw a flicker along the top of the divide and then another. They both knew what it was and fell into silence to watch. The northern lights flared high and white, and splintered on the snow.

Louise finally took an audible breath. "How terribly beautiful," she whispered.

"Yes," he said, looking at her again, with all the hope in his heart.

When the Ice went out in Febr.

9

The new year blew in more snow and strong winds. Erik fed the cattle, including Al's, in a horseshoe-shaped bend on the lower meadow, and kept a water hole open for them in the ice on the creek. The corral-like meadow was bounded by the creek and partly sheltered by cottonwoods and undergrowth along the bank. But the divide, into which the creek had eaten its way along here at one time, provided most of the shelter, a perpendicular bank seven meters or more in height.

Erik felt relief whenever he passed through the narrow entrance of this natural enclosure, escaping the wind with a load of hay from a stack in the open field. He drove around the bend close to the creek, scattering hay on the snow. White-faced cattle strung out after the hayrack, and munched contentedly on the green, sweet-smelling alfalfa. Erik carried out this routine regularly every morning and late in the afternoon.

Sometimes he also walked to the homestead farther down. He could cross the creek anywhere now on the ice, and he usually made it as far as the natural building site. From there he stood looking at the peaceful winter scene and across the whiteness to the Hills, and he thought about Louise. The only painful view was Gus's empty house. Erik never went near it.

One night Chris said to Erik, "I seen you across the crick a while ago when I rode by."

"Ye-es."

"I was wonderin' if some of the cattle was gittin' out."

"No."

"I didn't see any."

"I just went over to look at the homestead." But Erik couldn't even explain to himself; why he always felt so touchy about it–as if he felt a little ashamed–and had to be pushed?

"Figgerin' maybe you'll file on it?"

"I don't know."

"Wouldn't be bad," Chris remarked. "Somebody's going to take it one o' these days. That's a cinch. Close in and all."

"Yes," Erik tried to keep the idea going. "It looks all right."

"Well, if you want to see about it, you can go along, if you want, next time I drive up to the land office."

Erik nodded. "All right."

Chris mentioned it to Julia at supper.

"Well, that would be nice," she said.

Erik thought of writing to tell Louise. She had sent him a card with a winter picture of the canyon, pines loaded with snow, and rocks, bushes, and grass sprayed with ice from the waterfall.

In the spring she'd return, and they would be together again. All summer. Someday he hoped they could ride back to the canyon. Just the two of them. He lay daydreaming about it at night in the woodshed under his heavy quilts.

Meanwhile the short days passed by, one after the other, with winter hanging on. When the snow became soiled in the bend, storm clouds left a fresh layer like a clean tablecloth. And Erik drove back and forth, between the house and the bend, as regular as clockwork. He liked twilight best, when he left the bend to ride home over frozen tracks. The warm house with a hot supper waited for him, except on Sundays sometimes, when Chris and Julia hadn't made it home yet.

One such evening, when Erik drove out of the meadow he saw Al's car waiting in the middle of the section lane, and he drove his wagon into the road.

Al got out and strode over to him. "I seen you coming. I was up at Chris's, but they ain't home."

"No," Erik said, "they drove up the river."

"Yeah? Well, what I came to see about is if somebody couldn't go up to Jes's. I seen young Bates over at the post office this afternoon and he said Jes's cows was gittin' in his haystacks."

"Oh?"

"That's damn funny," Al continued. "Jes wouldn't let his cows in the stacks, would he? I figger maybe there's something wrong up there. Sick or something."

"The mailman didn't go on over there?" Erik asked.

"Naw. When he first seen them, he didn't think nothin' about it. That was Friday. He thought they'd just got out. Then he seen 'em again yesterday."

"Oh?"

"Yeah, it don't look good. He didn't see no smoke from the shack either. 'Course, you can't blame Bates. A mail carrier can't go and look up everybody when he's deliverin'. He don't come very close, you know. It adds half a mile or better, I guess, and he didn't have any mail for Jes."

Erik nodded, shivering hard.

"Well, I'd go up there in a minute," Al explained. "Only I can't drive in my car the way the road is up there, and I came over town 'specially to have supper with Miss Ainsley. Then we was going to church. I s'pose I could go back and try to find Fred, but I thought if one of you fellers could ride up there, it'd save a lot o' trouble."

"Yes," Erik heard himself say. "I'll go."

"I'd sure 'preciate it. Better take the team home first and git a saddle horse." Al started toward his car. "Oh, maybe it don't 'mount to nothin'," he added. "I'd just feel better if somebody rode up there and looked."

Erik hadn't seen Jes since Christmas at Mayland's. Jes had looked as thin and worried as usual and had coughed a lot. He'd asked Erik to come up, but with Louise home, Erik had neither time nor inclination.

Erik drove home quickly, unhitched, unharnessed, groomed, watered, and put the team in, and saddled and bridled Brownie. The sun had already gone down, but a half moon had risen, and with snow on the ground, it wouldn't get very dark. He rode Brownie across the iced-over creek and headed for the knolls. He began to wonder what he should do if Jes was sick. Mayland lived closest, if Erik could get through the drifts in the draw. What if Jes. . . . No, Erik couldn't think about that. If only he had somebody else to go along with him. Always having to go alone felt so hard, but it's what they all had to do out here. Everyone else seemed used to it. Erik supposed he'd get used to it too, after a while, maybe.

He kept Brownie trotting, but not very fast. Brownie didn't trot fast. Erik suspected Brownie moved just barely fast enough so it couldn't be called walking. He remembered how Louise sat perfectly relaxed at this gait, moving with her saddle, rhythm of horse and rider a perfect match. She could also ride Brownie bareback in that manner, as she often did, without ever tiring. Brownie was Louise's pony and would never be anybody else's. "Good old Brownie," Erik said aloud, patting the horse's neck. Even someone else's pony made him feel a little less alone tonight.

Erik didn't meet or see anybody along the way. A lone light glowed at Mat Burk's place. Through the curtainless window he caught a glimpse of a lamp on a table, with a dark figure sitting on the other side. Then he reached the wide section lane with its thin barbed-wire fence. No wind, only a cold draft drifted from the north, off the snow fields. Erik heard a distant coyote sound off with a long, drawn-out howl. The half moon beamed down white and clear, casting its thin light on the crusted snow.

Erik still had a mile to go just to reach the foot of the plateau. Why was he so conscious of every step of the way? So aware of moonlight glinting on the snow? The sheeted land reflecting the reflected sunlight. He felt like he was moving between two dead worlds, the moon and the earth. It was so quiet he imagined he could hear cold contractions of barbed wires.

Brownie slowed to a cautious walk at the approach to the slope. He tripped across the bridge over the canal and began the ascent. No tracks led this way, but the crust sparkling with moonlight was ice-hard. Gradually the wide expanse of the top opened up, a flat interminable whiteness reaching to the sky. Erik stopped Brownie for a moment to get his bearings.

He could just begin to make out the Hills and he turned south, keeping his eyes peeled for Jes's shack. He hadn't ridden out here for such a long time. The Hills steadily emerged over the edge of the plateau. At first he mistook the shack for a haystack, until he saw the galvanized flue sticking up, cold and gleaming, and then the corral fence. He rode down to the fence, dismounted, and tied Brownie to it. He finally realized the corral gate was open, and no cows were inside the fence. The closest hay stack stood on the north side, and Jes's cattle had knocked the snow off its sides, and some munched contentedly.

Erik thought about rounding them up, but he looked up at the shack, and he couldn't see any lantern light. He should have seen it through the west window, which only reflected the moon tonight.

Erik reluctantly crunched up through the pristine snow toward the steps, desecrating the glittering snow. He found clear tracks by the steps, but it hadn't snowed for several days. He stopped on the icy steps to listen and felt his heart pounding.

"Jes," Erik called. He was startled by his own voice. "Jes." He carefully moved up the steps and knocked, and the door rattled in the latch.

He glanced down the draw. Maybe Jes was out there looking for the rest of his cattle. Erik knocked again and slowly turned the doorknob.

"Jes," he repeated, with the door slightly ajar, and he tried to push it open.

The door stopped against something. The moon glared through the bare panes of the opposite window. Erik stepped up on the threshold to peer toward the bed, his shoulder pressing against the resisting door. He heard a creak and looked down, and at last he recognized the body slumped on its knees. Dark hair glinted in the moonlight against the edge of the door, and a rope led straight up to a two-by-four ceiling joist.

Erik slammed the door shut, leaped over the steps, and vomited into the snow.

Then he made poor Brownie thrash through the drifts in the draw, toward Mayland's.

Martha laid out food and tea while Mayland bundled up and went out and found Al and Fred. Erik sipped hot tea but didn't eat. The men quickly returned with Mayland to organize. A sleigh would bring Jes to Mayland's barn, Al would ride along and Erik drive, as long as he didn't have to look at the body again. Al removed the rope, hauled Jes to the sleigh, covered his frozen form with his own quilt, and tied him on the sleigh.

Later Erik, Al, and Fred rode back to round up Jes's dairy cattle along the draw, and drove them all the way to Chris's corral. Many were obviously pregnant. Chris shook his head. "Thanks. They'll be work." And that night had felt endless.

Erik went to bed near dawn, almost too tired to fall asleep, while Chris hammered loudly in his barn, building a second rough coffin. When Erik finally got up, he saw it tied on Chris's sleigh, along with two shovels and his crowbar.

Chris brought out the harnessed team and hitched them to the doubletree and the sleigh. "Come on. We have work to do."

Erik almost asked "What?" but he didn't want to know.

Chris drove them to Mayland's, where Mayland said the body had thawed enough in his barn to lay out in the coffin. Fred and Al arrived, and Al and Chris did that job. Chris had brought nails and his hammer to close the lid.

Martha put out food and tea for the men again, and Erik stayed inside with Mayland and Fred, sipping tea and eating supper. After Chris and Al joined them for a hearty meal, they helped hitch and load Mayland's sleigh with firewood, kerosene, and shovels. Al and Fred had each brought a pickaxe and a post hole digger, which they added to the sleighs. Then Chris and Mayland drove their sleighs to the cemetery, the rest of the men riding along.

All afternoon Erik, Chris, Al, and Fred had to dig a new lonely grave in the frozen ground. First they used shovels to scrape snow from the earth. They used firewood and kerosene from Mayland's sleigh to build a fire to loosen the frozen soil. They shoveled out the coals and softened dirt. They used pickaxes and post hole diggers, and Chris used his crowbar to loosen frozen dirt below, for more shoveling. Then more fire, as if burning a short ditch, and more shoveling and digging, and so on. It took a lot of work to put a coffin nearly two meters down in a Dakota winter.

Finally at dusk they laid out ropes near the hole, everyone carried the coffin from Chris's sleigh, they used the ropes to lower it down, tossed the ropes in with it, and shoveled dirt back in the hole, making a mound over it. At last the thin huddle of men in sheepskins, with no women at the burial, spoke a few words.

"Goodbye, Jes," was all Erik could say, wiping his eyes and his nose with his mittens.

Memories of those two nights would stand out starkly in Erik's memory, an inseparable part of the winter bleakness.

Later blustering winds blew without let-up, and Russian thistles rolled again across the fields and caught in the fences. Ragged days lengthened toward spring, and Chris and Erik went out to burn the ditches.

No one said much about Jes anymore. His death was something to forget about. People said it was too bad, but there was nobody to blame but himself. Life had to go on.

There were bound to be some wrecks. But that made Erik quietly angry, and the lonely image of Jes endlessly sawing wood trying to keep up, kept haunting Erik, like a bad dream. He remembered the afternoon they first met, Jes in his shabby suit with milk stains on his knees, sitting on Erik's bed talking about his plans. When Erik thought about Jes and Gus, Erik questioned his own plans. They suddenly seemed weakened by what had happened on both sides of him. Erik had always vaguely assumed that if men like Gus and Jes could make it out here, certainly he could.

Then one noon, coming in for dinner, Erik noticed a letter leaning against the clock. He seldom received any mail, but that was where Julia and Chris put it when he got any.

Julia saw him looking. "It's for Fred. It got in our box by mistake. Chris didn't notice."

"Oh," Erik said, disappointed, though it had happened before.

"Seeing it was from Louise," Julia added, "old Mr. Bates probably didn't even notice who it was for."

Erik didn't answer. He knew he needed to, to show he didn't care. But he only nodded and tried not to stare at the letter. It looked like a long one.

"Have to remember to send it along, next time somebody goes up there," Julia said.

Erik returned to the ditches and watched the weeds burn as black as his feelings. His eyes smarted from the smoke, and the Hills appeared distant and inky over the shoulder of the knolls.

He noticed the thick letter again that evening. He saw it the next morning and again at noon. But when he came in for supper it was gone.

"Fred was here this afternoon," Julia said after a while, looking at Chris. "He wants to go with you to the land office tomorrow."

"Oh? All right."

"I told him you'd stop by for him."

"Tell him I was goin' early?"

She nodded. "Yes, I said he better be ready."

Chris turned to Erik. "I was goin' up to the land office tomorrow morning. You still figger you'll file on that place, I s'pose."

Julia and Chris both looked at Erik, and suddenly he wasn't so sure anymore.

"I guess," he said.

"Because in that case you might as well come along," Chris continued obliviously. "As good a time as any, I guess. We ain't so busy right now."

"No-o."

A silence ensued.

"'Course, it don't make no difference to me," Chris finally added. "I was goin' up there anyway."

Erik nodded. He felt a heavy weight in his gut, the way he had felt the night he decided to take care of Gus's place. No, not decided–was pushed into promising to.

He lay awake a long time that night, feeling torn and uncertain. It seemed like nothing ever came easily for him, in the right order. He felt like he always had to make choices before he was ready. There was so much he couldn't know ahead of time. Fate was pushing him again and he was yielding. That was all. That was how he made all his important decisions, it seemed. Was it worth taking the homestead, if Fred took Louise? His heart felt broken.

"'Course, you'll have to stay down there," Chris said, on their way the next morning. "That's the hell of it."

"Ye-es."

"Part o' the time anyway. 'Course, you can always use the winters on it, puttin' in your time."

He made it sound like serving time.

"It ought to pay off in the long run," Chris added, more encouragingly. "A feller's time ain't worth a helluva lot in the winter anyhow."

Chris stopped in front of the post office and Erik ran in to retrieve their mail. He found Hayden standing by the service window.

Hayden looked up from a form he was filling out. "Just a minute here. I wanted to see you."

Erik removed the mail from Chris's box and waited. Hayden took his time, looking up from his form to talk with Mrs. Bates inside the service window. Erik leafed through the Dakota Farmer, and glanced nervously at Hayden and the front door by turns. After a little he stepped nearer the door to look out through the glass panel. Chris still sat in his car, with his eyes on the post office door.

Erik moved noisily back toward Hayden. "I guess I'll have to go," he excused himself. "Chris is waiting."

"Oh, I'm sorry." Hayden picked up his paperwork. "I thought maybe we'd have a little time to talk. But it can wait.

I just wanted to tell you I got a letter last week from a feller in Chicago, at the Art Institute. They held your sketch over for a showing of drawings and etchings, and he enclosed a clipping from one of the big papers. It mentions your drawing especially."

"Oh? It does?" They had accepted his drawing? His heart began to beat faster.

"Purdy good." Hayden nodded. "For a beginner. Of course, they realize you need more training, and they suggest you might apply for a scholarship if you want to."

"Oh?"

"Couldn't you come over some evening so we can discuss it? He also sent an application form."

Erik thought he heard the car door slam.

"You'll want to see the letter and the review anyway."

Erik nodded quickly. "Yes, of course." He headed uneasily toward the door again.

"You think it over," Hayden called after him. "I'll be seeing you."

Erik hurried out and saw Chris coming.

"It's about time," Chris said.

Erik handed him the mail.

"What the hell kept you so long?"

"Hayden was in there and–"

"Godamit," Chris cut in, and flung the mail through the open car window onto the back seat. "We ain't got all day."

Erik was about to walk around to the other side of the car.

"Godamit," Chris said again.

Erik suddenly stopped, and found himself whirling around to face Chris. "Don't you talk to me that way! I'm through being treated like a dog!" Or like one of Chris's poor frightened horses at the runaway.

Chris looked back at Erik, and started to move his lips, but nothing came out.

"I've slaved like a dog for you," Erik lashed out again, "but I won't be treated like one. By you or anybody else!"

For a moment they stood staring at each other.

"That so?" Chris said at last.

"I'm not going with you," Erik answered tensely. "Not anywhere." Why should it matter anyway, with that long letter on the mantle from Louise, for Fred? Why would Erik ever want to stay anywhere near here without her?

"Suit yourself, Godamit." Chris's eyes strayed toward the door of the post office. "Damn if I care. I got to git going–"

Hayden came out. "Hi," he called jovially, raising his hand in greeting.

"Hi," Chris replied distractedly.

"Sorry I kept you, Chris." Hayden walked over to the edge of the plank sidewalk. "Didn't know you were waiting out here. For a while."

"Yeah?"

Hayden looked from one to the other. "All dressed up, I see. Leaving town?"

"Yeah. Driving up to the land office."

"Yeah?" Hayden looked at Erik. "You too?"

Erik shook his head. "No."

"I dunno," Chris said. "He was gonna file on a homestead."

"That so?"

"No," Erik repeated.

They both looked at him.

"I changed my mind."

"I see," Hayden said knowingly. He turned to Chris. "Did he tell you?"

Chris glanced back at him uncertainly.

"Didn't he tell you about the letter I got?"

"Naw. Guess not."

"Well, I bet that's the reason," Hayden said, and he proceeded to tell Chris about the letter from Chicago.

Erik moved back to the sidewalk in front of the post office. The wind blew tacked-up papers on the bulletin board– auction notices in fat print, government announcements, and pictures of wanted persons: thieves, murderers, and escaped convicts.

"Want me to take you home then?" Erik finally heard Chris ask.

Erik shook his head.

"Better. It's quite a ways."

"I expect he wants to see me first," Hayden explained. "If you don't mind."

"Naw. That's all right. If he wants to. I dunno what he wants to do."

"We can go over to the shop for a while," Hayden said to Erik. "Might as well."

Chris paused, looking uncertain, and then got in his car. They watched him drive away, dust boiling up behind.

"He didn't much like it, I guess," Hayden said.

"I don't care."

"That's right," Hayden agreed. "You can't let someone else's opinion make any difference. When it comes to deciding what you're going to do with your life, you have to be the judge. Everybody has to figure that out for himself."

They walked together to Hayden's office, and Hayden brought out the letter.

Erik distractedly only half-read it.

"You get it all right?" Hayden asked after a while.

Erik nodded.

"Purdy good, isn't it? And here's the review." Hayden handed Erik the long clipping. "It's by Stevenson, you notice he says in the letter. One of the art critics."

"The drawing called 'Julia,'" Erik read, "is by a young artist from South Dakota. Technically it shows amateur lack of restraint in craftsmanship and too much concern with non-essentials, such as the landscape in the background window, which divides the attention somewhat. However, more experience and discipline can remedy these faults.

"More importantly, the artist has captured what is most essential. This is clearly not a simple studio exercise, but the face of a woman one feels was actually present in the flesh, as no doubt she was. It strikes the viewer as not only an honest representation, but an exceptionally mature one, showing in the eyes of Julia and in the lines of her mouth. One sees a sensitive, tender awareness of life, bearing down on an otherwise lively, almost child-like nature. This portrait is unmistakably promising."

Erik looked up from the review. "I didn't think the divide would do that."

"I don't know about that," Hayden said. "He could be wrong, I s'pose."

"I wish I had my drawing here. I can't remember."

Hayden deliberately unfolded the scholarship application form. "You're going to send it in, aren't you?"

"I guess. I don't know." Events were bearing down on Erik in their own relentless order again.

"Won't hurt," Hayden said. "It says here you'll also have to send along more of your portfolio. You do have more than the landscape?"

"Ye-es." Drawings of old shoes and cold horses. Would that work?

Hayden saw Erik's look and maybe misunderstood. "You don't have to agree to take the scholarship for school there, if they accept you, you know." He stuck the form in his typewriter. "Name," he read aloud and began typing.

"It's spelled with a k, not c," Erik said, watching.

"Oh yes." Hayden crossed out his start and made the correction. "Erik," he read. "I never noticed. It's the middle of America, isn't it? The word, I mean. With a c it would be perfect."

"It's a k over there."

"Oh? But I don't s'pose you'll ever go back. Not with the middle of America in you, I shouldn't think."

Erik looked past Hayden, out the window, at the false fronts across the street. "I don't know," Erik repeated firmly. He wasn't going to let anyone push him again.

Smoke still rose from the ditches and drifted across the field, like the smoke after a battle. Erik stood gazing tiredly through and over it at the homestead across the creek. Tonight the homestead looked different. It was not his as it otherwise would have been–if he had gone along with Chris today. So it seemed changed, as if he were seeing it after a long absence or as a stranger. Now he looked at it without the thought of possessing it, but his feelings still clutched at memories of it.

He had dreaded confronting Julia after his long walk home from town this morning, and he'd avoided her at first by returning directly to the woodshed. His doghouse, he thought bitterly. But then he had finally returned to the house to get it over with. He had said nothing about his tiff with Chris, but the news about his sketch was enough to explain why he'd come back.

"So this means you might leave us," Julia had said.

He had not thought of it so specifically in that way. He had felt it mainly as an assertion of himself. He wasn't sure where he'd end up, but he might at least leave this place if he wanted to, or if they didn't want him to stay.

Erik noticed a thin column of smoke rising straight up from the main ditch, at the approach to the flume. It looked like an offering in one of the old illustrated Bible stories. Some matted tufts of weeds and grass smouldered in the bottom of the ditch.

Gradually the column drifted up into the limbs of the cottonwoods and then began to thin out. Erik saw flames above the ditch embankment. Perhaps he had better go and check on it, and he picked up his pitchfork and a gunnysack. He stopped abruptly. The smoke wasn't coming from the ditch, and it was getting thicker and spreading. He started to run.

The fire had crawled around the end of the flume and ran under it, where the grass grew tall. Erik could hear hissing, and the smoke began to swirl. Flames already reached waist-high. He beat at their edges with his gunnysack but it only seemed to fan them. The center of the fire crackled and snapped in tangled undergrowth and leapt at bushes and saplings. He looked around helplessly and then stared back into the roaring fire. It drove him back, flames spreading in all directions, into anything that would burn. He scrambled back up the bank, coughing and rubbing his eyes. He needed help.

Erik glanced panic-stricken up the road. Chris should be back by now. He would see the fire. Smoke now towered in the sky. Flames already licked at the timbers of the flume, and its tin trough crackled in the heat. In desperation Erik dashed down the bank again and tried to drive the fire back, but it leaped out fiercely and scorched his flailing gunnysack.

Erik tore his way through the bushes to the creek, and dipped the gunnysack in it. Just to do something. If only he could find a discarded bucket or something to carry water. But he found nothing, nothing useful–only some rusted-out tin cans. The fire rose like a wall. And he moved back. He had to move back.

Flames engulfed the girders from side to side, enveloping the whole spidery structure. He had no chance of saving it, and he stepped farther back from the steady, concentrated roar. The smoke actually diminished, and suddenly a brace cracked. A charred, flaming arm struck out sideways, and hung for a moment from its lower abutment before dropping straight down. The trough began to sag in the middle. Then it cracked. In the next instant one of the girders gave way, tearing the framework apart. The whole structure swayed momentarily, broke, and then collapsed in a tangle of burning timbers and twisted rods, while sections of the trough plunged to the ground and shattered.

Erik tore up the bank, his side aching, and heard voices at last.

"Get the axes!" Chris called to Fred. "Have to try to keep it from spreading!" Chris struck out along the bank, and Erik followed him.

Fred came running with buckets and axes.

"Cut a path right down through here," Chris directed. "Just git the worst of the brush out in a hurry and start a fire from this side. The three of us oughta be able to hold it."

They all went to work clearing a swath to the creek, and then they started the backfire. It ate slowly and steadily away from them. They had filled the pails with water but didn't need them. Chris left to see if the fire was spreading on the other side of the flume. But he soon returned to report it had already gone as far as it could, and had died for lack of fuel at the junction of a deep gully.

"A wonder the ditch rider don't come," Chris added. "A feller ought to go up there, I guess, and have him turn a head o' water on. Then we can flood the whole damn bank."

"Yes," Fred said, "but why didn't we think o' that sooner?"

"Oh, it'll take several hours for the water to git down here, but I have a notion to go by and tell him. This is gonna smoulder a helluva long time." Chris turned to Erik. "You better come along, I guess. Then we can stop back at home for supper and git the chores done."

"Sure," Fred volunteered, "I'll stay."

Erik didn't say anything, preparing for the worst. He should have watched the ditch fires more carefully. This terrible event was all his fault. Another runaway.

"You ain't hurt?" he heard Chris say.

Erik finally realized Chris was asking him. "No."

"Well, we better take a look when you git your clothes off." Chris turned to go.

"I'll pay for the flume," Erik offered to his back.

Chris whirled on him. "Hell no! You ain't gonna pay for it. It weren't your fault–ain't nobody gonna pay for it. Serves 'em right, if they can't keep the weeds out o' their damn ditches."

Surprised and confused by Chris's changed attitude, Erik rode with him in silence. What if Erik didn't get the scholarship? As Hayden had said, he couldn't count on it, and now he couldn't count on water for the homestead either, if Chris wanted him here. Should he flee or stay here, but if he ended up with neither choice, what could he do? What if he tried to stay for Louise, and she went away with Fred? Erik's thoughts circled and circled, not knowing where to go.

10

On the Fourth of July, Chris's family, Al, Hayden and Erik all sat in front of the family tent after supper, facing the water. They'd picked a level spot near the widest part of the reservoir, about halfway between the dam and the inlet to the west. A few other families had also pitched tents, scattered around a larger tent set up for dancing later on. Erik studied a miscellaneous collection of vehicles, from flag-decked cars and buggies to box wagons and hayracks, and even a covered wagon, all parked around the fairgrounds. An impossible drawing.

Family groups ate or cleaned up after picnic suppers, while children darted in and out with lusty shouts and squeals between intermittent bursts of firecrackers. Yet Erik still felt a bit let-down after the earlier commotions of horse races, calf-roping, steer-riding, and bronco-busting. Fred was still out there among the cattle pens, helping to pack up stock before he joined the crew setting up fireworks. Erik caught Louise also gazing in Fred's direction, after looking at the dirty dishes on the picnic blanket and her mother's silent expectancy with disgust.

Hayden took out a letter from his pocket, unfolded it, and waved it at Erik to get his attention. "You got it!"

"What?"

"The art scholarship in Chicago! Do you want it? What shall I write them?"

Louise finally faced Erik. "You should take it!"

Erik almost stubbornly said, as he had many times, "I don't know." Why did Hayden have to tell everyone? But Erik's heart suddenly leapt, and he said instead, "Let me read the letter."

Hayden handed the letter to Erik.

"Well, what do you think?" Al asked impatiently, while Erik read slowly to himself, his hands shaking with excitement.

At last he looked up at everyone sitting in a circle on the picnic blanket, but Louise stood up and turned away.

"I want it–I do want it!" Erik said. He'd just made one of the fastest big decisions in his life, without being pushed. "Tell them, Mr. Hayden. Please tell them for me." Erik could finally leave the hard work, loneliness, and suffering of Dakota, and learn how to do the work fate meant him to do. Meanwhile he actually felt like celebrating with everyone tonight.

"This was a good idea," Al interrupted Erik's thoughts, "celebratin' the Fourth up here. Lots o' room for the kids to play and swim. Nice clean fun for everybody. Just let yourself go, by golly, and forgit everything. Seems like old times."

Chris swatted resoundingly a mosquito on the back of his hand.

"I seen Mat Burk on the way up," Al continued, "and asked if he wasn't going too. 'No,' he said, shuttin' his mouth tight as a trap. He wasn't goin'. He was too busy, the sonofa–" he caught a warning look from Julia. "The sonofagun."

"Well," Julia said, "maybe he wouldn't enjoy it as much as you do."

"Naw, 'course not. That ain't the point. It'd be good for him. To git away from himself once in a while. That's what it's for, ain't it? That's why we're shootin' the works."

"Well, that's sort of a loose interpretation, I guess," Hayden said.

"Darn right. That's what this country needs. Cut loose once in a while. That was the trouble with Jes if you ask me." Al shook his head. "Just got himself tied up in a knot and couldn't git out."

"You needn't be so literal," Hayden objected.

"It's a fact, ain't it?" Al countered. "That's the way it is with a lot o' people. 'Course, Mat won't kill himself, I guess. He takes it out on somebody else. Ever tell you about the time his plow wouldn't scour?" He looked around their circle. "Well, sir, he got so gol-darn mad he went home after his shotgun and killed it."

"The plow?" Julia exclaimed.

"Darn right." Al beamed. "Unhitched the horses and tied 'em to the fence and just let 'er have it. Both barrels."

"You seen it?" Chris said.

"Naw, but by golly that's what they say."

"I don't doubt it." Chris shook his head.

"Darn tootin'. Another time he took a pig that was gittin' out o' its pen and sawed it in two on the barbed wire, right in the middle. To teach it a good lesson, you know. So the pig wouldn't do it anymore."

"Well, that's enough now," Julia said. "Don't tell any more."

"Gee whiz, I was just gittin' started."

"That's what I was afraid of."

"Holy gee-whiz."

"Unless you have something nice," she compromised.

"Naw." Al shook his head. "That don't make good stories."

"I don't see why not."

"It just don't, that's all. I guess everybody has such a heck of a time that the only thing that makes 'em feel good is hearin' about somebody that's worse off."

For a moment nobody spoke, and Hayden took out a cigar and lit it.

"I seen Gus the other day," Al finally spoke up again.

"You did?" Julia said, looking interested.

"Yeah. I was up in the Hills, and suddenly I seen him walkin' ahead o' me. I thought it was him, and sure enough that's who it was, all right. You wouldn't know him hardly. Course, he just came out o' the mines. Looked like the devil."

"Did he say anything?" Julia wanted to know.

"Naw, not much. I walked along with him to the place he lives. It's upstairs over a kind of second-hand store, I guess it is, an old ramble shack building held together with iron cramps, and it had long, black windows. It looked so bleak I didn't go in."

"What did he say?" Julia persisted.

"Oh, I asked him how he was gittin' on, and he said, 'All right, I guess.' He said he was tryin' to save enough to go back to the old country. It seems his folks is still livin'. I sure felt sorry for him."

"I don't know why it is," Julia said sadly, "some people have so much bad luck."

"It's true," Hayden said. "I don't know if it's fate, but we get pushed around some."

Erik nodded.

"Sometimes it seems there isn't any justice," Julia added.

"No indeed," Hayden agreed. "Of course, our sense of justice is naturally a little biased."

After a pause, he explained, "We take a narrow view of things, you know. We judge things by the values we happen to have, whether they're any good or not. You were just saying, Al, that Mat Burk was too busy to come here. Well, what was he busy with? That's the question. Something more important?"

"Hell no! Just more work on his crops, which are never gonna amount to anything with all that damn alkali. Might as well take a day off, and maybe find a wife at the dances here."

"But he thought his farm was more important," Hayden said. "He's got his sights set too low maybe, but who hasn't?"

"And," Julia sighed, "I don't s'pose anybody can put his sights, as you call them, so high that he can't also be hurt."

Erik shivered. He told himself once more that he would have to let go of this. Take one dream instead of another. Why did it have to hurt?

"I guess so," Hayden sadly agreed. "But I think the trouble with us is we're so close to the ground. A child begins to advance himself by crawling. And when he does stand up after such a long time, it's with somebody's help, and within easy squatting distance from where he started. By that time he's already had a lot of experience reaching for things. And that's about as far as some ever get. All they want is something to touch, something within reach, something they can easily get their hands on. The trouble is that what they want isn't always right there. So they run the risk of being disappointed all through life, and finally they are, of course."

"Well," Al said, "I'm not sure I know what you're talking about anymore. Seems to me you're gittin' off the subject. I thought we was talkin' about Mat and Gus."

"We are," Hayden said. "Or people just like them. People who can't see anything except what's right in front of them, who don't care for something like this even, coming up here on a holiday."

"Naw," Chris said, "there sure ain't much to come for either."

"I don't know about you folks," Al said. "I've had a good time. I'd've been sick stayin' home by myself, knowin' all this was goin' on."

"Is it just for things like this that we're living, do you think?" Julia said, turning to Hayden.

"Well, I think we're a little closer to the truth here," Hayden said. "If you think back, it's something like this you remember longest, a trip to the Hills for no other reason than to be there, or just a moment when you forget yourself for something else–" he broke off, to look up at Louise. "Are we missing a lot over there?" he asked her.

Louise had taken several distracted steps towards the reservoir. She straightened her skirt and brushed it off, not answering him.

Hayden shrugged and turned his attention back to Al. "You were telling about the way Gus lives now, down in the mine all day and a grim rooming house to come home to. And I suppose his life down on the crick wasn't much better. I've known a lot of fellers like that. When I was on the paper up in the Hills years ago, I remember I wrote an editorial about it. I used the old proverb, 'All that glitters is not gold,' and added, 'even if that's what everybody calls it.'

"Most of the readers were miners of course. And what they were after was gold. That's what they'd come to the Hills for. They worked in the rocks and dust, and that's what they actually got, mostly. Some of them live out here now, and when they return to visit the Hills, it isn't to the mines, but some nice picnic spot or mountain scene, or maybe all the way to Harney Peak."

"You bet." Al nodded. "It's purdy nice down there too, or up there, maybe I should say."

"You remember the granite intrusions?" Hayden continued. "Tall rocky shafts stabbing out of the Hills? There's a row of them in one place. One evening like this, I saw them looking like tall tapers on a stone altar, with dark pines below. If you've ever seen them once, you can't forget them. It's high there, you know. I turned to look out over the slopes below, ridge on ridge in a purple sea to the horizon, fifteen, twenty miles, I guess. Maybe more. That's not what the prospectors were searching for. That's not something they could pick up and put in their pockets. But if any of them ever saw it, that's what they'd remember."

"Yeah, that's all right," Chris said. "But you can't live on it. The feller that don't have anything can't even go up there and see it."

Erik couldn't help trying to catch Louise's attention by looking at her, remembering the evening they'd watched the sunlight crown the granite turrets. But she stood as if waiting to go somewhere, her head turned towards the water.

"If it wasn't for this irrigation dam here," Erik heard Chris say, "what d'you think the valley would look like? There wouldn't be anybody hardly."

"By golly, it'd be a damn sight better," Al spoke up. "That's what's the matter with this country, too damn crowded."

"For heaven's sake," Julia broke in, "let's not get started on that."

"For heaven's sake is right," Hayden agreed.

"Well, there ain't nothin' you can do about it anyhow," Chris added.

"Naw," Al replied. "But it don't make no difference. Someday this damn pond is gonna fill up with mud anyway. That'll fix it."

"Well," said Hayden, "maybe it's just as well you aren't in charge of it. We have to make a living, as you say. But it's easy to make the mistake of thinking that because a little is good, a lot would be better. Yet we can't be satisfied with any less than we can imagine. But one life is all we have. Maybe we don't get what we try for, but we don't get any more. That's certain.

"You watch people when they're not looking, or listen when they're talking like this, and you'll soon find they're settling for less, and secretly longing for what they might have aimed for. It's not the getting but the trying that finally counts."

"You hear that, Louise?" Julia asked her.

"What?"

"Weren't you listening? What are you staring at?"

"By golly," Al exclaimed, "look at that sky, will you!"

The dipping sun set the sky aflame from side to side, and the lake mirrored it. Erik stood up. He'd already made his decision about what he could reach for, what he was meant to do, and he knew he wouldn't find it easy. It never had been. But he told himself he wouldn't ever flee from it again.

"You think you could paint that sunset, young feller?"

Erik shook his head at Al's question. He just felt ready to learn how. He watched Louise walk towards the water.

"Nossir," Al said. "You can't beat it. You sure can't."

Erik was about to follow Louise.

"I guess you'll leave this country purdy soon," Al stopped Erik with the remark.

"Ye-es."

"Not leaving it exactly," Hayden observed. "I guess he'll take it along."

"By golly, he better not!"

"You have to get away from this place, you know, to possess it," Hayden explained himself. "If you stay here it'll possess you instead."

"You don't say."

"And it doesn't take much, you know," Hayden added. "Only about six feet."

Erik edged away from the circle, and Louise finally glanced back when she heard him approach.

"You know what it looks like?" she said.

"What?"

"A cloud with a satin lining."

"Yes," Erik said. "Too bad it won't last much longer."

"But it's getting prettier all the time. I've been watching it. Look at the lake, shimmering in different colors and ruffled across the middle."

The sunset cast a rose reflection on her face and arms. "I'm glad we drove up here. Aren't you?"

"Yes." He wanted to say more, to touch her, to have someone to hold on to. Even though he knew it was too late, perhaps from the very beginning. It took all his strength not to reach out to her one more time.

"I know you have to go." Louise kept her blue eyes on the water. "I've suspected it for a long time now. But you'll always remember us, won't you?"

"Yes, I'll always remember you." He swallowed hard.

"Look," she said. "You were right. It's already darkening."

"Well, come on kids," Julia called. "We're going, I guess."

"Yeah," Al's deep bass joined in. "I'll need some help foldin' this tent."

Erik took Louise's arm lightly, she turned to him, and said, "And the night shall be filled with music."

"Yes," he said. "Go on."

"And the cares that infest the day

"Shall fold their tents like the Arabs,

"And as silently steal away." Louise smiled sadly.

Then all Erik could hear was the water lapping on the shore, and he tried to let it all go. He needed to. He had to.

Harvest came early, and they threshed directly out of the shocks to get as much done as possible before Erik left. A drought came, hitting especially hard on the range, where both pond water and feed became increasingly scarce. Fred had to continuously move the herd westward toward Broken Rock. Finally he rode home, leaving Joe to look after the cattle for a few days. Fred and Chris promptly decided to bring the cattle in and keep them on the divide and the unclaimed homestead, until after the third cutting of alfalfa. They sent Erik down to repair the section of fencing destroyed by the flume fire.

Fred stopped by on his horse while Erik stapled the last length of barbed wire onto the new posts he'd set.

"Sure did a good job of it," Fred observed. "The fire, I mean. Just about cleaned this place up, didn't it?"

"Yes." Erik glanced at the charred remains of one of his dreams. Soot coated his shoes and the cuffs of his overalls.

"They're not going to rebuild the flume, I hear," Fred said.

"No?"

"Naw, it wouldn't be worth it, with what little there is to irrigate over there. I don't know why they built it in the first place. Just standing there rotting and not doing a damn bit o' good as long as there's nobody on the homestead."

"No-o," Erik said.

"So they're going to open it up as a dry claim, they say."

Erik nodded.

"Wouldn't be bad," Fred said. "Purdy good pasture, good bottom land, and plenty o' water."

Erik nodded again, seeing it coming.

"If they want to do the right thing," Fred continued, "cut it off from the project, I mean, I think maybe I'll file on it. Might as well, I guess, before some damn honyocker beats a fellow to it." Fred paused, and looked across at it. "I guess you figured on taking it once."

"Ye-es. I–" don't call me–Erik had to bite his lip.

"Before you decided to leave, I mean."

"I was thinking about it," Erik said. "I still am," Erik added, just to scare him.

"Yeah? Been all right too." Fred looked frankly at Erik. "Louise tells me you got a scholarship to study art."

Erik nodded, swallowing his own words.

"That's all right. You must be purdy good, I guess, to get it. I was kinda hoping you'd stay and settle down."

"Oh," Erik said, forcing a smile.

"They're going to miss you, I know. Louise was telling me last night what good times you've had. I was almost beginning to wonder if she was going to back out on me." Fred laughed. "Naw, but seriously, she sure appreciates you.

Thinks you been mighty swell to her. She's an awfully nice girl, isn't she?"

"Yes, she is." Erik pounded hard on the last staple.

"I guess I'm purdy lucky. I don't know what I was thinking about. Rita was all right—I don't mean that. But anyway, Rita's married now and happy, I guess."

Erik nodded yet again. Maybe he wasn't the only one fate pushed around.

"That's the way it goes." Fred sighed. "'Course I've known Louise a long time, ever since she was a kid. For so long everybody expected us to end up together, but for a while I just wasn't sure. But I'm glad now it turned out the way it did. I'll feel different about her, and I really do love her." Fred paused again. "You think she'd be happy over there?" He nodded in the direction of the homestead.

"Yes. I'm sure." Erik sighed. Another possibility gone. Did Fred even deserve her?

"Yeah? Well, that's the way I feel too. Close to home and all. But I better get going, I guess. About noon, ain't it?" Fred nudged his pony. "I'll be seeing you."

Erik watched Fred ride away, and then Erik turned to load his fencing tools in the wagon and climbed on up. The horses, tired of standing so long, set into a trot towards home.

Erik couldn't help wondering now what it had all meant. Had whatever he had hoped for with Louise existed only in his mind? Something he had spun his world around, like a web, and just as fragile? Louise could not have known of the many hours, days, and months she had filled Erik's thoughts. Had he simply played an entertaining background part in her existence, like the slopes and the Hills, or the sagebrush she loved, or the ride in the snow, watching the northern lights over the divide?

He glanced back at the homestead, and the natural terrace at the foot of the divide, as it had existed through all the ages before he had come here. A haze lay on the Black Hills. From up there this was only a gray streak on the horizon, somebody had said long ago. Just like the homestead looked from Chris's. Erik turned the wagon into the road, rutted and hard, and the jarring of the wheels went straight to his temples.

On his last Sunday in Dakota, Erik went to say goodbye to the old folks. He felt like he was repeating his first day here. Sunlight from the west window fell across the table and pooled on the floor. Again he listened to the tinkling of porcelain and silver, and the language of the old world Mayland and Martha always spoke when they were alone. Erik had not really seen them much, but they had remained on the edge of his consciousness, providing a refuge where he could always go when he needed to. Like the night he'd fled from Jes's shack.

"It's been nice having you here," Martha said, holding out her pale hand to him. "You seemed like one of our family."

Erik could see Louise in Martha again, in her profile and her blue eyes. Martha smiled. Yes, Erik thought, she was wonderful, as Louise had said the night they drove home for Christmas in the sleigh over the snow.

Mayland followed Erik out. "Well, it doesn't feel very long since you arrived here. I remember we was standing right here when Chris came. I can still see you two driving up the curve."

"I remember," Erik said.

Mayland held out his work-hardened hand to Erik. "Well, so long, and let's hear from you once in a while."

"Sure."

And Erik rode up the curve alone. He checked in next at Hayden's office, but he wasn't in. At the post office Erik learned from Mr. Bates that Hayden was out of town and would not return until the end of the week.

So Erik wouldn't get to see Hayden again before he left. Erik nodded, and started for home. On the way he rode past the two graves on the hill, Anna's small granite stone by itself, and a little to the west the wooden cross with Jes's name on it and two words, "At Rest." At rest above the worries and toils of his life. At rest overlooking the Hills, blue and aloof across the horizon.

The next day Chris asked Erik to begin hauling wheat to the grain elevator, probably to raise money for his accumulated wages. And the last morning Chris took a load himself. Erik watched from the barn door, and then turned inside to saddle Brownie for Louise, who planned to spend the day with her grandparents. He felt a bit relieved that she wouldn't be here when he left. He would watch her ride toward the creek and then across the bottoms, as he had done so many times before. As he slowly buckled Brownie's bridle, the barn door opened. Louise stepped just inside the barn, as fresh as always, her light hair glowing like sunlight in the half-darkness of the barn.

"So it's goodbye," she said as she approached him.

He stood looking at her. For the last time. The idol of his dreams, in the fields, on his lonely Sundays, in the night under his musty quilts.

"I'm sorry," Louise said, and suddenly put her face up to his and kissed him on his lips. How soft and tender her lips felt, and yet how much pain they gave him now.

He gripped her arms, to keep her from pulling away.

"What do you want?" he demanded softly. "Do you want me or Fred?" He couldn't help asking.

"You must leave, and I can't." She shook her head.

At last he let her go, forever. He heard her sniffling as she led Brownie out. She stood against the open doorway and waved to him. And then the barn door swung shut and the light went out.

He stepped back into Brownie's stall so he couldn't hear her ride away. He had to remind himself that this day too would come to an end, as his trapped tears finally spilled out. By evening he wouldn't be here, but speeding along the foot of the Black Hills away from Dakota at last.

His bed had not been made when he returned to the woodshed. There was no point in it. Julia would put the sheets and pillowcases into the next wash, and she'd fold up the quilts and put them away in an old trunk, where they'd stay until another hired man needed them. Erik dusted off his suitcase and began packing.

"I don't see how Chris will get along without you," Julia said at dinner.

"Naw," Chris agreed.

To Erik it didn't seem any different from all his other dinners with the two of them. Afterward he dried the dishes while Chris took his nap.

However, Chris got up soon and went outside to load more grain, and when they were ready to go, Julia came out to the wagon to say goodbye. Erik saw her still standing there as they drove away.

At the gate Chris offered to get down. "You might git something on your suit."

"No," Erik said, "I'll be careful."

Chris drove through, and Erik closed the gate. He paused for a moment with his calloused hand on it, looking back.

"Anything wrong?"

Erik shook his head and climbed up.

Chris glanced at him and then busied himself with the lines. They crossed the bottoms in silence, except for Chris's spasmodic attempts to make Sally pull up. At the top of the knolls Erik turned again, to look back for the last time at the little house on the divide. "Goodbye," he said to himself. Then they drove over the hill to the basin flecked with alkali. Erik could make out the roof of Gus's house, as leaden and dead as the divide.

Chris turned the wagon off toward the train station as soon as they crossed the tracks, and he stopped at a row of hitching posts opposite the loading platform. He handed

Erik his suitcase and then got down and tied the team up before walking with Erik to the platform in front.

"Well," Chris said at last, "I s'pose I can't do much good here." He held out his large, firm hand. "Goodbye and good luck."

"Goodbye."

Erik met Chris's eyes, which glistened too. Then Chris turned around and didn't look back.

Erik stood watching him drive away toward the grain elevator. Then he moved his suitcase against the station wall. He already had his ticket. Here he was at last. How many times Erik had looked toward the station, yet how different it felt, now that he was truly leaving. Perhaps it was the difference between wanting to flee, and having a destination.

"Goodbye Dakota." He heard the distant wail of the train–an engine followed by two yellow coaches and a baggage car coming across the flats for him. But this place would never become just a gray streak in his memory, and the sound of the train didn't feel nearly so lonely anymore. When Erik finally boarded, his heart glowed with memories and hope.

The End

AFTERWORD

I don't know when my grandfather, Hans Holst Andersen, wrote this novel, although it must have been sometime later during his lifetime (1894-1962). Like Erik, he immigrated through Ellis Island at age 18, knowing only Danish, and earned his way on South Dakota homesteads. Yet he earned a degree in English and French at Iowa State Teacher's College (now University of Northern Iowa), he earned a doctorate in Philosophy from the English Department at the University of Chicago, taught English literature and composition, and became head of the Department of English, Foreign Languages, and Speech at Oklahoma A&M (now Oklahoma State University).

He submitted this novel only to one publisher, it was rejected, and he died relatively young compared to his many Danish sisters and brothers. So the manuscript was handed down to his younger son, my father, who handed it on to me, and I admit I have taken some liberties with it! So what have I done? Although my grandfather's language was surprisingly modern, I changed many passive verbs to active verbs, and substituted some common words more appropriate for this story in the place of some more sophisticated professorial words. I have also given this novel a subtitle to clarify the title.

I suspect my grandfather indeed traveled from Oklahoma back to South Dakota to visit and photograph his old haunts. That explains why his photographs fit his story so well. "Miss Ainsley" is not "plump, dark, and lively" in her picture, because I used a winter portrait of my grandmother, who in fact played Christmas carols on her grand piano for her family to sing along.

I also clarified a few awkward sentences and passages, probably due to an author writing in a second language. I also studied horse-drawn plows and their harnesses in order to fill in details to help the modern reader (and myself) understand a crucial scene, "the runaway." Finally,

I tried, although not completely successfully, to stick with this novel's vocabulary throughout.

Now I come to "P.C." "Honyocker," in case you haven't already looked it up for yourself, it was indeed a derogatory term for Scandinavian immigrant homesteaders. Lastly, Harney Peak was the historical name in the era this novel takes place (early 1900's), but thank goodness it was finally renamed Black Elk Peak in 2016. (Harney was a commander who massacred Sioux warriors, women, and children at the Battle of Blue Water Creek. Truly awful!) Lastly, my grandfather seemed to have an unusually early sympathy for women, Native Americans, and the environment. Wow. Not to mention immigrants, he among them.

Now, how about quotations? He must have known about or maybe even read "All is fair in love and war," first found in John Lyly's Euphues (1578) or in the novel Frank Fairlegh by Frank E. Smedley (1850). In this same novel is "All that glitters is not gold," a derivative of a line in William Shakespeare's play The Merchant of Venice, which employs the word "glisters," a 17th-century synonym for "glitters." He must have also read The Good Earth by Pearl S. Buck (1931), and then presciently, he somehow came up with, "The Sound . . . of Silence" (1964) Simon and Garfunkel, and "Purple Haze"(1970) Jimi Hendrix. Amazing.

Next, I discovered my grandfather must have been a man of his times, with a stiff upper lip, which included his novel. Here's a clue from his book: "Mama took it pretty hard." (Anna's death.) But "Papa can stand it better. Because he's a man, I guess." My grandfather hid most of Erik's feelings, even though Erik's conflicted emotions are crucial for this beautiful gem. So I had to infer most of Erik's feelings, for which I found many clues, and I wrote them in. I also wrote a few short scenes I think my grandfather found too painful to write.

Granddad also skipped *completely over how Erik made his Big Decision.* It just happened between scenes. Unbelievable! I could not let such a wonderful book pass over this vital plot point; character conflict and change. So once again, I had to do my best to find a respectful way to insert it, in the right place, without interrupting the flow of the story. I hope I achieved this.

Now for a bit of Family Lore. Why did my grandfather immigrate from a large Danish family that moved from one struggling farm to the next? Our family story was "He came here to avoid conscription by the German Army." Not true, according to a talk I had with his youngest sister in 1990! Great Aunt Didda told me he came here "for opportunity." According to my parents, his novel is "Largely autobiographical." Reportedly he did start out here as a young man with no English on South Dakota homesteads.

My dad said his father talked about riding a horse out there and carrying a gun to kill rattlers. My dad remembered visiting with him a grateful old man at a dugout. My mom said "Some girl turned him down." If he had to leave a blond girl, he married instead my redheaded grandmother, Pauline Waits. Grandmother said "He carried my books," when they met in college, after he'd made enough money to leave the homesteads. I was also told that he became a U.S.

citizen by joining the U.S. Army. He became a signalman, and WWI ended a day before he reached the front, where he would have been a prime target. So that is why I'm here, with my red hair.

My last but most important word. Having dug deep into this novel multiple times, I got the strongest feeling and conviction that although I know my grandfather began his American life in South Dakota, *my grandfather was really here in this book. He must have lived this.* He wrote so instinctively, bringing his characters alive, with such vivid and sensory details and settings, he must have lived through this! It must be true. It's difficult to believe now that he wasn't a struggling artist. Actually he did become an artist, with words. Is that how he left South Dakota? I think he borrowed the rest from one of his brothers.

Anders Andersen made his living in Denmark as a painter and sculptor, after his family somehow managed to send him to art school. Hans also sent his old clothes back overseas to his brother. When I met granddad, as a very young girl, he had no accent. Awesome! Oh the questions I wish I could ask now! Did my grandfather climb up to the rocky turrets? Did he walk the flume? Did he have to live alone in a woodshed and in someone else's dugout? Did he find the body of a despairing homesteader? Was he too upset by it to bring himself to write a reaction and burial details? Did he finally tell off his boss? Did he witness the flume fire? Did a young woman foolishly scorn him in South Dakota? But forget any questions. My grandparents are buried side-by-side in Stillwater, Oklahoma. May they rest in peace.

A Little Bit More....

I did some digging into historical documents, and according to his WWI draft registration card my grandfather actually worked as a "farmer" for Nis Sorensen, in Nisland (named for Nis because the town was founded on his land in 1909), in Butte County, South Dakota. Sound familiar? Mayland–Maybe-Land?–Make-Believe-Land? Nis—Chris?

Presumably Hans escaped the 1918 flu by living in such a remote, under-populated, rural area. He was described as tall, slender, blue eyed, and light haired on his draft card. Oh, and by the way, I have lighter red hair than grandmother's. Everyone in my family, except my mother, was tall, slender, and a version of blond. We were all born with blue eyes but mine turned green. And so his genes pass on. I caught the writing bug, as you might guess. Many thanks for your interest in this story.